THE TALE OF

DRAGONS AND FLATFEET

Book 3 of the Ella Trilogy

CATARINA HANSSON

AuthorHouse™ UK
1663 Liberty Drive
Bloomington, IN 47403 USA
www.authorhouse.co.uk
UK TFN: 0800 0148641 (Toll Free inside the UK)
UK Local: 02036 956322 (+44 20 3695 6322 from outside the UK)

Because of the dynamic nature of the Internet, any web addresses or links contained in this book may have changed since publication and may no longer be valid. The views expressed in this work are solely those of the author and do not necessarily reflect the views of the publisher, and the publisher hereby disclaims any responsibility for them.

Any people depicted in stock imagery provided by Getty Images are models, and such images are being used for illustrative purposes only.
Certain stock imagery © Getty Images.

This book is printed on acid-free paper.

ISBN: 978-1-7283-7949-4 (sc)
ISBN: 978-1-7283-7950-0 (e)

Print information available on the last page.

Published by AuthorHouse 05/19/2023

authorHOUSE®

Also by Catarina Hansson

The Tale of Oknytt and Gray Gnomes

The Tale of Gealdors and Runes

In Swedish

Tigerspår

To my grandchildren

Contents

An ending begins ix

Names in the Ella trilogy xi

Notes on the Aesir faith xiii

Ella's family..xiv

What happened in The Tale of Oknytt and Gray Gnomes and The Tale of Gealdors and Runes xv

1   The Beacons are on Fire! 1

2   Ditch, Smoke, Soap, and Water 6

3   Moose Ride and Dragon Food.. 12

4   The War Starts.. 15

5   A Dragon Awakes 19

6   Dragons and Gray Gnomes 23

7   Jarl Olav.. 27

8   War Strategy.. 31

9   Dragon Cave 35

10 Breakfast 40

11   Silje Town...43

12   Birk's Plan 48

13   The Attack on Nifelheim 51

14   Jarl Olav and the Ellacross 54

15   Attack and Defence 59

16   Birk Is Coming 63

17   Tora, Nidhugg, and the Flatfeet..67

18   An End and a Beginning 71

19   Queen Tora 74

Words to know...79

An ending begins ...

Welcome to Nordanland, where a girl called Tora lives with dwarfs, giants, humans, and elves. But there live also bad people and creatures like oknytt and gray gnomes. Have you ever seen a gray gnome or an oknytt? No, they're not very common here, but there are a lot of them living in Nordanland.

Oknytt are rather short creatures with long, floppy ears. They have small, black eyes and yellowish skin. As soon as anyone approaches, human or animal, they become virtually invisible—the oknytt can blend into their surroundings for brief moments, and this ability makes them excellent thieves and spies. Oknytt are vicious but fortunately quite gullible.

The gray gnomes are also quite short, but muscular and strong. They each have a very large nose with which they can track down most things. That's why they often work on finding things and sometimes even people.

I thought I'd tell you a little about mountain giants. They live up in the mountains and prefer to be left alone. The worst thing they know is humans and dwarfs—why, no one knows. But they find it hard to grow enough food in the cold mountains, so they sometimes work extra as soldiers. They are very big and strong and get angry easily, so you must know what to say to keep them calm.

The mountain giants' favourite animal is the mastodon, a large elephant with a furry, thick coat. Mastodons like the cold and snow up in the mountains. Their tusks are thick and can grow as long as four or five metres. When a mastodon comes clattering, it's best to stay away.

The Flatfeet lives far away in Lawland. They are quite short but muscular and they all have long black hair, very blue eyes, and big ears and they all look almost the same—same hair colour and hairstyle, same clothes, almost the same facial expressions.

We can't talk about who lives in Nordanland without mentioning Tora, who is the main character of this book. Tora is a young girl who is a seid. A seid can see into the future and help the sick. But is that all she is? One day everything changed for Tora. What will happen now? I'm not going to reveal that to you here, but for now you can read about Tora's adventures in peace and quiet.

Names in the Ella trilogy

Ash, Soot, Black	three ravens
Atte	a Black Elf
Birk	an evil sorcerer who is not allowed to live in Nordanland
Botvid	a gray gnome
Brage	an evil, not-so-good magician who works for Jarl Olav
Egil	a king of the dwarfs who rules in Nifelheim
Elgur	King of the Elks
Ella	Tora's mother, a strong seid who was queen of Nordanland before her death
Grandmother	**Lin,** a seid, deceased mother of Queen Ella and grandmother of Tora
Grim	dwarf
Jarl Olav	The self-proclaimed king of Nordanland, who is stingy and mean
Nariin	Queen of the Elves
Nidhugg, Bluetooth, Crimson, Fire, Oak, Sable	dragons
Odin	the most powerful god in the Aesir faith
Sigrid	a powerful seid who is leader and chief of Fala village, and sister of Tora's grandmother
Solve	Tora's late father, who was king of Nordanland
Thor	god of thunder and weather in the Aesir faith

Tora	a seid and healer, daughter of King Solve and Queen Ella of Nordanland
Trolgar	a gray gnome
Truls	a magician and healer in the town of North Island
Viva	sister of Tora's grandmother, a seid and magician
Wolf	Tora's companion wolf
Wolfpelt	leader of the oknytt

Notes on the Aesir faith

Odin is the leader of the Asgardians. He is the god of warriors, can see everything that happens, and is very wise. Odin has two ravens, Hugin and Munin, and the horse Sleipner, which has eight legs. Valhalla is Odin's castle where he receives Vikings who have died in battle.

Thor is, among other things, the god of thunder and the protector of mankind. He is strong and rides across the sky in a chariot pulled by goats. Thor's hammer is called Mjölner.

ELLA'S FAMILY

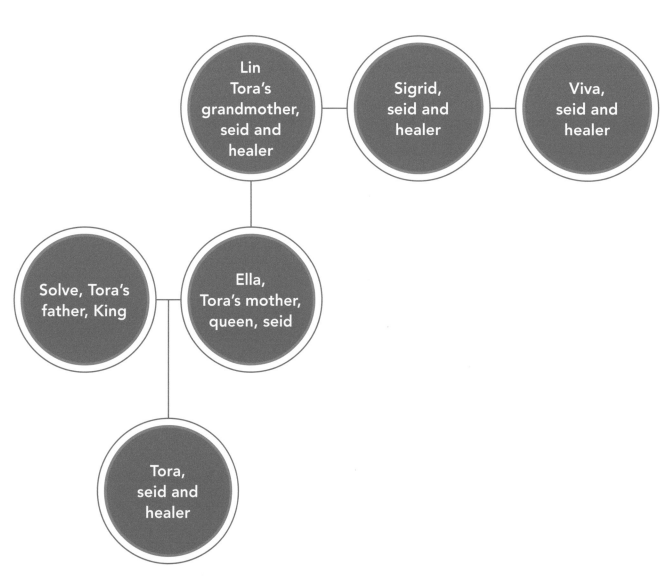

Lin
Tora's grandmother, seid and healer

Sigrid, seid and healer

Viva, seid and healer

Solve, Tora's father, King

Ella, Tora's mother, queen, seid

Tora, seid and healer

What happened in The Tale of Oknytt and Gray Gnomes and The Tale of Gealdors and Runes

Tora is an orphan girl who has lived with her grandmother for about eight years. One day, the villagers came for her grandmother because she was accused of being a witch. Tora then leaves the village and goes into the forest. There she finally gets help from her grandmother's sister Sigrid. Tora, her grandmother, and Sigrid are all strong seids and healers. They can do things such as see into the future, dream true dreams, cure certain diseases, and talk to animals. Sigrid's other sister, Viva, is a strong, blind magician who lives alone in a cottage in the forest. Viva tries to teach Tora everything she can.

Jarl Olav has made himself king of Nordanland. He kidnaps Tora and burns down Fala village where Sigrid is the leader. The people of the village flee to the dwarfs' cave Nifelheim and gather a large army to free Tora. Tora tricks Jarl Olav and his magician Brage and manages to escape from the castle in the town of Silje to Viva's cottage in the forest. There she stays for the summer with her best friend, Wolf.

Tora is given an enchanted ellacross by Sigrid and Viva for protection. The gealdor, spell, attached to the cross makes it smell bad when an evil person comes near Tora. A long time ago, the god Odin gave several ellacrosses to the seids to use for good deeds. Now both Jarl Olav and the gray gnomes are very keen to have some ellacrosses so that they can become rich and powerful.

Time stands still in Viva's cottage, and Tora suddenly discovers that autumn has come to the Ancient Forest. Viva says that a blood moon is approaching and warns that evil forces may grow stronger. Just then there is a knock on the door of the cottage and an elderly, hunched-over man with a long, white beard enters. A faint foul smell spreads through the cottage, and they realize they are visited by a dangerous man. Viva offers the mysterious man tea while Tora and Wolf prepare to leave the cottage. Before they go, Viva slips Tora the last nine ellacrosses in the world. Viva is bewitched by the mysterious man but survives.

Nifelheim, the dwarfs' great cave city, is attacked by oknytt, who manage to take over the cave. Their leader, Wolfpelt, seizes the dwarf throne. Egil the Dwarf King lures him into the dwarfs' treasure chamber, where Wolfpelt is trapped with two dragons. The dwarfs take over Nifelheim again and prepare for war against the evil forces that are on their way.

During the oknytt attack on the dwarfs, Tora manages to escape. She makes her way to the town of North Island where she joins forces with Truls Healer. She is soon joined by Wolf and the ravens.

The mysterious man who bewitched Viva turns out to be Birk Witchmaster, who was banished from Nordanland for many years. Birk takes over Silje Castle and rules over Jarl Olav by means of powerful dark magic as he plots evil deeds.

Meanwhile, the gray gnomes make another attempt obtain the ellacross but fail. On the outskirts of Nordanland, the enemy gathers at the Lake Mimir's Well and prepares for battle.

1

The Beacons are on Fire!

Sigrid wakes up with a jolt, still tired. She has only slept a few hours in her room in Nifelheim, the dwarfs' cave village. But what has woken her? She hears people running in the corridor outside and the clatter of metal. Sigrid opens the door and sees dwarfs quickly making their way out, armed and in armour.

"What's going on?" she asks a passing dwarf.

"The beacons are on fire!" says the dwarf, looking stressed. "Now it's urgent!"

Sigrid gasps. The beacons that line the hilltops to warn when the enemy is coming are on fire. Someone is attacking Nordanland. So now is the time. Birk Witchmaster has gathered his army and is ready to take over the country. With the help of the power of the blood moon, he may succeed. *Well, that makes two of us, you old moth-eaten witch.*

Sigrid goes to the great hall, where soldiers are picking up weapons, people have brought food parcels to be loaded onto carts waiting in the yard, and soldiers are saying goodbye to their families. Sigrid feels a terror strike her heart, and she takes a deep breath.

As she walks out of the big gate, a pigeon swoops down and lands gently on her shoulder.

"Express mail," says the pigeon, holding out the letter in its claw.

"Thank you," says Sigrid, taking the letter. "Can I ask you a favour?" she asks the pigeon. "Can you fly to the town of North Island and look for Tora? Tell her she must come home."

"Absolutely," says the pigeon and flies away over the treetops towards North Island.

Tora and Truls sleep soundly in the wide window frame of the shop in the town of North Island. They have read all about dragons in the book Viva gave Tora. Now Tora is flying high above the ground on a beautiful, golden-red dragon, and the wind of speed is sweeping through her long hair. She wakes with a jolt to the ringing of the bells in the watchtowers around the town.

Truls sits up and rubs the sleep from his eyes. "What has happened? Is there a fire?" he asks in a daze as he looks out at the square.

"I don't know," says Tora. She feels a cold lump of fear spread in her stomach.

Wolf enters through the back door. "We must leave. The beacons are on fire," he says, looking serious. "We must go home immediately."

"Okay," says Tora, running into her room to quickly gather her things.

"Don't forget the things you put away," Wolf calls after her.

"No, I won't," says Tora. *Obviously, the wolf has smelled its way to the hiding place under the floor,* Tora thinks as she pulls out the package with the only ellacrosses that is left in the world from its hiding place under the floorboards. She puts them in her bag along with the book about dragons that Viva gave her.

"I'll go with you if it is okay," says Truls. "We can use all the good forces we can get together. Besides, you might need some help with the dragons."

"Yes, of course you can come along, but don't expect any dragons," says Tora. "I've never seen or heard of any dragons in Nordanland."

They quickly pack up some food and drink, grab the walking sticks leaning against the wall by the door, and set off. Truls locks the door and says a silent prayer to the god Odin that he will be able to come home again one day. The friends walk down to the ferry as the ravens fly high above them in large circles. This time, Wolf doesn't have to swim across. He is allowed to go on the ferry without anyone protesting.

The ferry is soon full and leaves the island. When it reaches the halfway point, there's a gasp and a flap as a pigeon lands a little too hard on the deck next to Wolf.

"Ouch," gasps the pigeon, getting up wearily.

"How did it go?" Wolf asks kindly, looking at the dishevelled bird.

"Good, thanks, but it was a long flight into the wind," sighs the tired pigeon. "I'm looking for Tora. Do you know where she is?"

"Yes, she is right behind you," says Wolf.

"I'm Tora," says Tora, picking up the tired bird. "What can I do for you, my friend?"

"Sigrid says you must come home," gasps the pigeon. "The beacons are on fire."

"Okay, thanks, we are already on our way," says Tora and puts the pigeon down on a blanket. "You'd better rest for a while."

"Thank you," says the pigeon, blowing up its feathers so that it looks more like a ball than a bird. Then the tired bird goes straight to sleep.

Tora looks worriedly out over the lake as the ferry glides closer to shore. What will happen now? Who is attacking Nordanland? Is she really going to see a live dragon? It would be both terrifying and absolutely amazing. Thoughts rush through her head, almost making her dizzy.

Meanwhile, Sigrid searches for Egil the Dwarf King. He stands and inspects the troops as they head north towards Lake Mimir's Well. Egil looks tired and worried.

"A day of sorrow, Sigrid. May Thor's thunderbolts pinch the enemy's butt!" Egil snarls angrily.

"Be careful what you wish for," laughs Sigrid." Suddenly it might hit home. Do you know why they lit the beacons?"

"Yes, the elves who guarded the border to the north decided to light them when mountain giants riding mastodons came to Lake Mimir's Well. The mountain giants are making some money now that Birk Witchmaster needs their help."

Mountain giants live up in the mountains and prefer to be left alone. The worst thing they know is humans and dwarfs—why, no one knows. But they find it hard to grow enough food in the cold mountains, so they sometimes work extra as soldiers. They are very big and strong and get angry easily, so you must know what to say to keep them calm.

The mountain giants' favourite animal is the mastodon, a large elephant with a furry, thick coat. Mastodons like the cold and snow up in the mountains. Their tusks are thick and can grow as long as four or five metres. When a mastodon comes clattering, it's best to stay away.

"Mountain giants! I haven't seen a mountain giant or mastodon since I was a little girl," says Sigrid, wondering. "I think I'll go to the cottage in the Ancient Forest and talk to Viva. I'm sure she can give us some tips and advice."

"Viva came here a while ago with Pail and Silver, the white elves," says Egil. "You'll probably find them in the kitchen."

Sigrid goes to Nifelheim's big kitchen. It is full of people preparing and packing food for the soldiers. In the middle of the mess, Viva and the white elves sit drinking tea.

"Hello, Sigrid!" calls Viva. "I've poured you a cup of tea."

"Hi," says Sigrid and sits down with a sigh. As usual, Viva knows what's going to happen before it actually happens. "You know why I need to talk to you?"

"Yes, we know," says Silver. "We also got words from our Queen Nariin that our best scouts are looking for the dragon Nidhugg. We hope he's still alive and can help us."

"That's great," says Sigrid. "What does Nariin want me and Viva to do?"

"You will ask Tora to awaken the dragons under Silje Castle. They have slept long enough, Queen Nariin says. We'll take Viva home with us so the queen's healer can help her recover from Birk's spell. That was a strong and evil gealdor," says Pail and anxiously looks at Viva.

"Good. Viva, take it easy and do everything they say, and you'll be back on your feet in no time," says Sigrid, patting Viva's hand.

"Of course, dear," Viva replies with a pale smile. "You must help Tora with the dragons, even though they probably already know she is coming."

"How should we do it? They might be a bit grumpy when they wake up," says Sigrid with a giggle.

"They will recognize Tora," says Viva. "Give them dragon lily, jungle flame, and burning nettle when they wake up so they can get their strength back. Then ask the dragons to help us end the fighting quickly and take care of Birk Witchmaster once more."

"Let's go and get you some help, Viva," says Pail. The beautiful white fabric runs like water around her body, and the pattern in silver keeps changing.

Viva gets up and gives Sigrid a hug. Sigrid thanks the white elves with a bow, and the group walks through the crowd, which parts and bows deeply as the white elves pass by. Sigrid can't stop the tears streaming down her cheeks as Viva disappears out the big door.

No, this won't do! Sigrid pulls herself up. *Now let's see if I can remember where the dragon lily, jungle flame, and burning nettle grow so I'm ready when Tora gets home.* Sigrid leaves the kitchen to help find and bring the plants for the hungry dragons.

Ditch, Smoke, Soap, and Water

The smoke from the enemy campfires blows out over Lake Mimir's Well. Thousands of trolls, oknytt, gray gnomes, and mountain giants have gathered around Lake Mimir's Well and in the forest nearest the lake. The enemy army is now so large that it cannot fit in the fields around the lake. Trees must be cut down to provide both firewood and more space.

The thousand-year-old spruce tree that the elves Lof, Nal and Non had been peering out of for the past few days was cut down yesterday. A thousand years of life was ended in an hour by two mountain giants with big axes. The elves luckily escaped and are now sitting in a tall tree a little way into the forest. They can only watch as the enemy destroys the Ancient Forest.

Suddenly something happens in the enemy camp. The forest becomes completely silent as the birds stop singing. The only thing heard is branches snapping as something large makes its way through the forest. The soldiers stand silently waiting, all looking in the same direction. The ground shakes every so often, and the oknytt cower whimpering.

Then it comes into view, the biggest mastodon anyone has ever seen. It has beautiful long fur that flutters in the wind and huge tusks polished to a shine in the sun. Perched on its back, Birk Witchmaster sits on a big black and gold throne, high above the ground and all the soldiers. He has left the castle in Silje and come to meet his new army. The mastodon walks toward the middle of the large camp, not caring what or who it steps on, and stops at Birk's signal.

Birk Witchmaster raises his hand, and even the wind dies down. The whole area becomes completely silent, as if nature is holding its breath. Everyone stands still and quiet, waiting for the witchmaster to speak.

"Soldiers," Birk calls out in a dark voice. "Today is the day we've been waiting for. Today is the day we take power over Nifelheim and Nordanland and make all dwarfs, humans, and elves our slaves." *And I take all the gold in Nifelheim,* Birk thinks and smiles.

The cheers that erupt hurt your ears and never want to end. The soldiers around Birk seem almost enchanted by their leader. Birk raises his hand again and everyone falls silent immediately.

"Kneel before your leader!" he shouts, and all the soldiers immediately fall to their knees and bow their heads.

"Now is the time to hurry," says Lof up in the tree. "I will run as fast as I can and let the others know. Do what you can to delay and disrupt them without risking your lives."

There is a crack in a tree a little way away, and they immediately fall silent. They look silently between the branches and then relax. More elves have come to help, and down on the ground stand Grim Dwarf and Atte Black Elf. Non, Lof and Nal quickly make their way to the ground.

"Greetings," says Atte Black Elf, and both Grim and Atte bow deeply. "We brought some help when we went this way." \

There are several elves around them, but they are barely visible because they blend in so well with the forest. Some of the elves scout into the deep forest so that no gray gnomes or oknytt are nearby and can eavesdrop.

"We don't know what the army wants, but we can assume that Birk and his magic has something to do with it. We have some ideas on how to stop the enemy a bit, to slow the army down on its way through the forest, until we know what's going on," says Grim, looking a little sly. "It might even be really fun."

"Say, do you have *fertilizer* in your plan?" Nal asks, holding her nose. They look at each other seriously for a second. Then they start laughing as they remember what happened at Silje town.

"Yes, but only as smelly smoke. We also have water and ditches," says Grim, who can't help but look pleased. "Our friends have already prepared everything."

"Let's go and see what you've come up with," says Non, patting Grim on the shoulder. "This should be interesting."

They walk back a few kilometres in the forest. A long, deep ditch that wasn't there a few days ago comes into view. The deep ditch winds through the forest, right where they usually walk to Silje. Down in the ditch, people are digging and carrying away dirt, gravel, and stones to build a big wall on the other side of the ditch.

Behind the wall, large throwing machines have been built. Next to the machines are barrels of water. Lof, Nal and Non who have been sitting in the tree watching for weeks and had no idea of all the preparations made, are impressed.

"Impressive! Tell me, how will all this now stop Birk's army?" Nal asks as she curiously looks around.

"We believe that the enemy army will move as fast as it can through the forest towards Silje town. They think that we dare not meet them here in the forest, so they won't send out any scouts. But we'll be on the lookout, of course, and if they have scouts, we will catch them before they have time to warn the army," explains Grim.

"We're about to fill the ditch with water from the river," says Atte. "Then it will be muddy and slippery. We expect mastodons and mountain giants to have great difficulty getting out of the ditch once they have fallen into it."

"As you can see, we have built a wall along this side of the ditch. Behind the wall stand our throwing machines. They will fire at soldiers on the other side of the ditch, coming from further back and to the sides," says the elf in charge of the ditch work.

"What should we throw from the machines?" Non asks, a little afraid of the answer.

"Water and birch soap," laughs Grim. "There's nothing worse for a troll and it smells good."

They laugh at the idea that big and dangerous trolls actually run when they get soap and water on them. They walk on to the end of the ditch where huge piles of branches have been gathered.

"These big bonfires are supposed to produce thick smoke that smells very bad," explains an elf. "We reckon the smoke will make some soldiers not see the ditch and fall in. The smoke will sting the big noses of the gray gnomes and make their eyes water, so they don't see where it's going and fall into the ditch."

"What will make the smoke smell bad?" asks Nal and smiles. "Which animals have you now asked for help?"

"Dried dragon manure," says Grim and looks pleased. "Burning dragon dung smells worse than skunks, according to Sigrid."

"Dragon manure?" Nal looks at him in surprise.

"Believe it or not, there is a very large mound on the other side of the mountain behind Silje Castle," says Grim. "Smelly and ready to be used."

"Now it's time to fill the ditch with water," says one of the workers.

Muffled whistles spread along the ditch, and it quickly empties of people. After a few minutes, Grim hears a faint hissing sound. Soon the first rivulets of water come along the bottom. Within minutes the water is high in the ditch, and the friends look on with satisfaction. They hope it will stop the mastodons for at least a day.

As they prepare for battle in the forest, Lof has run at breakneck speed to Nifelheim to tell them that the enemy is on the move. Lof comes running into the great hall where Egil the Dwarf King sits with his leaders. Breathless, Lof leans against the table and delivers the message. The enemy is now moving towards Silje and Nifelheim. Egil thanks the elf and asks him to eat and get some rest.

"My friends, it's time," Egil says, and they go out to the soldiers who have not yet left.

3

Moose Ride and Dragon Food

Tora, Truls, and Wolf sleep under a big fir tree, tired after hours of walking without rest. Tora dreams again of dragons, fire-breathing and dangerous, sweeping down on New Fala village, and she has no time to escape. The dream disappears, and a dragon's head appears, blue-green with great scales glittering in gold. The dragon has a narrow braided beard and warm, golden-yellow, friendly eyes. Suddenly the dragon says, "Greetings, Tora!"

The dream feels so real that Tora feels the dragon's breath on her cheeks, but for some reason she is not afraid.

"My name is Nidhugg, and I am the emperor of all dragons. You may have heard of me. I knew both your grandmother Lin and your mother, Queen Ella. Now that they are no longer on earth, you are our new Dragonmaster, our leader and queen, and I need your help. Witchmaster Birk is starting a war against Nordanland. You must awaken the dragons under Silje Castle. Only can they end the war quickly before too much is destroyed. They are waiting for you, and Sigrid knows what must be done. I will return to Nordanland soon with help." The dragon disappears, and Tora sleeps on, calmer than she has been for a long time.

Wolf wakes up, stretches his stiff legs, and yawns loudly. He crawls out from under the heavy branches and is met by four long grey legs.

"Good morning, Wolf," says a dark voice above him.

"Good morning, Elgur," says Wolf. "It's been a while." Wolf looks up at the old moose, who is grey around his nose and have friendly brown eyes. "Everything all right?"

"It would be a shame to complain," says the moose. "The leaves are green, the water is clear, and the sun is shining. We hear you're in a hurry to get back to Nifelheim and Silje. Thought we might be able to help."

"That's very kind of you," says Wolf, bowing. "I'll wake my travelling companions immediately." Wolf crawls under the branches and says, "Time to wake up. We've got a long way to go and we're in a hurry, so I thought we'd set off at moose strides."

"Moose strides?" asks Truls. "Well, we'll have to take big steps, Tora." Truls laughs.

Tora and Truls crawl out from under the branches and are met by four stately moose.

"Good morning, Tora," says the old moose and bows. "My name is Elgur, and I am king of the forest moose. We offer you our help."

"Good morning," says Tora and bows. She doesn't really know what to do when she meets the king of the forest, but a bow seems appropriate. "Thank you, that's very kind of you."

"Moose strides," says Wolf and laughs, pleased with his joke.

Tora and Truls climb onto their respective moose and head off towards Nifelheim at tremendous speed.

The animals with the long legs move quickly and easily through the forest and it's not long before they reach the beautiful dwarf village. Tora and Truls slip off the moose and bow in thanks. The large animals disappear back into the forest, almost silently despite their size.

Tora sees Sigrid standing next to four wagons loaded with large baskets full of plants. Truls and Tora walk over the grass to Sigrid.

"There you are," Sigrid says happily. "Welcome! Truls, it's been a long time since we saw each other, to long." She greets her old friend with a big hug. "Thank you for taking care of Tora during her time in North Island."

"Hi, Sigrid," says Truls. "It's been fun and educational. She knows a lot already and learns quickly, whatever it is. You've been busy, it looks like," says Truls, looking at the plants in the wagons. "I can guess who's going to eat this."

17

"What is it?" Tora asks. "I don't recognize any of the plants."

"This is dragon lily," says Sigrid, holding up narrow green leaves with bright stripes that grow together like a small umbrella. "It blooms with a beautiful burgundy flower, but it smells like rotten meat. Terrible smell, but dragons love both the flower and the leaves."

Sigrid goes to the next trolley. "This is burning nettle, and you must wear gloves when picking it. It burns and then itches for hours afterward. Dragons like it best when it has grown big and become a bit tough in the stem and leaves. No dragon will do well without burning nettle in its food, no matter what kind of dragon you are feeding."

"Finally, we have jungle flame," says Sigrid, holding up branches covered in dark green leaves. "On some branches you can see small yellow and orange flowers. They grow as tall shrubs but don't like the cold, so we grow them in special rooms at the white elves. Without jungle flames in their food, the dragons can't breathe fire."

"Why do we have all this food for dragons?" Truls asks. "Are we expecting visitors?"

"Nidhugg will be here soon." says Tora, "He wants me to wake up the dragons that are asleep in the mountain behind Silje." She looks at Sigrid. "You know what I'm supposed to do, don't you?"

"Has Nidhugg visited in a dream perhaps?" Sigrid laughs. "Dragons prefer to talk without words, you see. They speak with telepathy. Then they can talk to you in the distance. Well, the dragons will be hungry when they wake up, but I'm sure Truls will be happy to help with the feeding."

"But first, *we* need to eat something!" Sigrid puts her arm around Tora. "Then I'll get the gealdor I need to wake the dragons. I'd better get it right, so they don't get annoyed. A newly awakened, grumpy dragon is nothing to play with."

The three friends go into Nifelheim to rest and eat a little before going to the mountain behind Silje.

4

THE WAR STARTS

The enemy at Lake Mimir's Well blow war horns that echo over lake and forest. Birk Witchmaster sits atop his mastodon and watches contentedly as the great army slowly begins to move into the forest towards the town of Silje and Nifelheim. Once and for all, he will take the power over Nordanland and Nifelheim, and lock Tora and Sigrid in dark dungeons. He can already picture himself in the great treasury of Nifelheim, looking at all gold and diamonds that is his, only his. King Birk.

He lets most of the soldiers go into the forest before he himself sets out. He must stay far from any fighting and keep his back clear in case things go wrong and he needs to escape. His memory of his last attempt, many years ago, to take power in Nordanland and Nifelheim still stings. He turns red in the face with anger just thinking about it. Queen Ella and Sigrid were lucky that time and managed to defeat him only because they had the help of the old dragon Nidhugg.

But not this time. It is a blood moon coming and he has already power over Jarl Olav and the castle in Silje. Also, Birk has made sure that Nidhugg can't help. He has placed a powerful gealdor over the dragon that only a very skilled elf can remove. The dragon lies old, sick, and weak in a cave, unable to move. He will starve to death because he cannot go out to get food. Birk sits and enjoys his chair as he thinks about the sick dragon.

Further into the forest, elves, dwarfs, and humans together lie in wait on the other side of the newly built wall. They hear the war horns honking and pat one another's shoulders encouragingly. Together they will stop the enemy. The bonfires are lit, and soon heavy smoke billows into the forest. The stench of burning dragon dung begins to spread, and it is not pleasant. All the soldiers along the ditch wrap cloth around their noses and mouths to avoid the worst of the smoke. The throwing machines are loaded with leather bladders filled with soap and water, ready to shower the trolls.

The first enemies are rapidly approaching the ditch, eager now that the attack is finally underway. First come the multitudes of oknytt, making their way smoothly through the dense forest. They cough and snort at the smoke, and their eyes mist up so they can't see where they're going. They fall into the ditch and splash around screaming in panic.

After them come the mastodons with mountain giants to lead them. The mastodons are frightened by the piercing screams of the oknytt from the water. The large animals begin to hurtle through the forest straight into the ditch, dragging the mountain giants with them as they try to stop them. The panic worsens as the big animals slides into the water, pushing the oknytt under the surface. The mastodons cry desperately as a warning to the other animals.

Behind the mastodons and oknytt come hundreds of gray gnomes lumbering through the forest. They hear the screams but don't understand what's happening. The thick smoke doesn't help. The stench of burning dragon dung gives them nosebleed—and when a gray gnome's big nose bleeds, it *really* bleeds.

The gray gnomes try to escape the smoke by turning back, but there are more gray gnomes, oknytt, and trolls heading their way. As if the forest isn't messy enough, large leather bladders filled with soapy water start raining down on them. The big trolls howl in terror, flail wildly, and start running back in panic to get away from the water as the bladders hit them and burst.

Birk hears howling and shouting a little way into the forest. At first he thinks his army has already encountered the enemy and is now winning the first battle. But he soon realizes that this is not the case. The mastodon he's sitting on hears the warning cries of the other animals and responds with a deafening trumpeting. Birk covers his ears, but it doesn't help. The mastodon's trumpeting is so loud that he can't hear anything for a few minutes.

Suddenly there is a crash in the forest in front of Birk. To his horror, he sees how his army has turned and now comes rushing back towards him in panic. The mastodon he sits on rears up in terror, turns with a jerk, and rushes back towards the lake. They are followed by oknytt, gray gnomes, and trolls in one blissful mess. Birk is thrown by the mastodon but luckily manages to latch onto the top of a spruce—otherwise, he could have been trampled to death by everyone now running in panic under him as he dangles from the spruce.

Eventually the forest calms down, and Birk pulls himself up into the spruce to observe. He sees that his army has gathered at the lake again. The mastodons stand a little way out in Lake Mimir's Well, ready to leave again at the slightest sign of danger, just in case. *I think I'll stay here for a while.* Birk takes a deep sigh, safe in the top of the tree.

At the ditch it is chaos. The smoke is thick, and the stench makes it hard to breathe. On both sides of the ditch, oknytt and gray gnomes are sliding around in the mud or struggling to get out of the water. The mastodons trumpet through their huge trunks in panic. The sound is so loud it hurts the ears of everyone around. The big beasts can't make it up the slippery edge of the ditch even with the mountain giants pulling at their reins for all they're worth. Suddenly, one of the mastodons rushes off along the ditch into the water instead. Oknytt and gray gnomes throw themselves away in panic to avoid being trampled to death by the large, panicked beast. The other mastodons see their friend running away and quickly decide to follow. They rush after, leaving the oknytt bobbing in the waves behind them.

Some oknytt and gray gnomes manage to get past the newly built ditch and wall under cover of the thick smoke and chaos. They walk quietly further into the forest and gather in a clearing well away from the battle. There they wipe off the mud as best they can and give their sore eyes a rest after the smoke.

As the day progresses, more oknytt and gray gnomes gather in the clearing. They sit quietly and rest, waiting for new orders. After a while, Trolgar the gray gnome looks at his friend Botvid, clears his throat, and says quietly, "I suggest we do something that can be useful for us when the fighting is over."

"Who made you a leader then?" Botvid the gray gnome snarls as he stuffs his nostrils full of moss. He's very tired of constantly getting his nose full of stench from Tora and skunks. This latest smoke was terrible, and he won't walk another metre without his nose stuffed full of moss.

"Shut up!" Trolgar the gray gnome hisses in reply. "If you have a plan, feel free to take over. No? Then listen. We're going to find Tora and steal the ellacross from her once and for all. Then *we* can be the rulers of Nordanland." The gray gnome stretches proudly. He can almost see himself as king standing on the walls of Silje Castle.

Botvid looks at Trolgar and nod. It sounds like a good plan. Botvid sighs, thinks of the stench around Tora, and tears off another tuft of moss.

5

A Dragon Awakes

Five elves stand looking at the mountain that rises high and proud before them. Snow lies at the top all year round, but down here green grass and dense moss cover the black-gray rock of the mountain. Low trees and bushes grow here and there, and mosquitoes buzz hungrily around their heads.

"Are we in the right place?" asks one of the elves doubtfully. "I don't see a cave."

"It's here. Queen Nariin is always right," replies another elf. "Keep in mind that Birk Witchmaster has put a strong gealdor over the dragon and the cave. We must search carefully."

The elves spread out in a sparse line and begin to slowly walk up the mountainside. They look carefully at bushes and trees for the faint glint of fairy dust that can sometimes be seen from a gealdor.

When they are about halfway up the mountainside, one of the elves suddenly calls out. "Here! See how it glitters on the leaves of the big bush." The elf points to a rather large shrub that does indeed glisten faintly in the sunlight.

The eldest of the elves walks up to the bush, raises his hands to it and says three times:

Hauta! Unar hauta hosta nildo!

(Stop! Nothing stops a friend!)

Suddenly everything goes quiet. The wind drops, the birdsong dies down, and the elves stand as if in a bubble of silence. Then the glistening fairy dust slowly begins to lift from the leaves, round and round and upwards in ever faster swirls, until with a little poof the elf dust is gone. Now that the gealdor is gone, the elves see a large cave opening.

"This is it," the old elf says quietly to the others. "Bring the dragon lily and the burning nettle so we can feed the old dragon as soon as he wakes up. A hungry dragon at dawn is no laughing matter."

Three of the elves quickly run down the mountain to fetch the large bales of dragon lily and burning nettle that they brought with them from their homeland.

The elves light the candle lamps they always carry in their belts and walk slowly into the great cave. The cave is pitch-dark, and the light from the small lamps is of little use. Large black spiders crawl and cling everywhere. Their webs are hanging thick and sticky from the walls and ceiling, and the elves slash their way through with their swords. The spiders are so numerous that they immediately mend the webs behind them. The faint rattle of all the spider legs follows them as they walk deeper into the darkness.

Suddenly the cave opens into a large hall. There are cobwebs hanging across the hall. At the far end is a very large stone completely covered in cobwebs. The elves can hear the dragon's heavy breathing, but they cannot see him. They spread out in the cave, but all they see is cobwebs. They stop at the giant stone at the far end. The stone is completely covered in the thick cobwebs.

"Quiet!" says one of the elves. "The breaths are heard more clearly now."

The elves stand still and listen. They hear deep, quiet breaths behind them. They spin around and look at all the cobwebs covering the big rock.

"Maybe this isn't a big stone after all," says the old elf. He starts removing spider webs carefully with his sword.

The other elves start to tear at the net, and soon they see a piece of the dragon's skin. They continue to pull and tear at the spider's web as the spiders gather around them like a black wall of hairy bones and bodies.

Soon the elves can see the big nostrils on the dragon's nose. When they have freed about half the dragon, he moves a little and takes a deep breath.

"Look out!" shouts the old elf. "Don't stand by the head!"

The elf who first freed the dragon's nose from the cobwebs has just enough time to jump away before the dragon sneezes. Fluid and sparks shoot out of the nostrils and land on the spiders a short distance away. Anything hit by the dragon's liquid melts away in a second. The other spiders panic and try to get out of the cave. In the panic and mess, they trample one another. As the spiders fall to the floor, they disappear in glistening dust—they were yet another evil gealdor cast by Birk Witchmaster.

The dragon snorts under the spider's web. The old elf clears his throat and says nervously, "Take it easy, noble Nidhugg. We'll free you as fast as we can. We ask you to lie still for a while longer so we don't stab you by mistake."

The dragon understands and lies perfectly still, neither sneezing nor snorting. The elves tear and hack at the spider's web, and soon the dragon is free. He lies perfectly still but opens one eye. He looks carefully to see where the elves are before lifting his head.

"Oh, it is good to stretch a little!" the dark voice of the dragon rumbles in the cave. "Many thanks, my friends, for your courage and help."

"We come with greetings from Queen Nariin. We've brought you food."

"I have been talking to the queen while I have been resting," growls the dragon. "Heard Birk is busy and causing trouble again."

"Yes, the world needs your help once again," says the old elf, worried.

"Then we don't have time to stand here and talk," says the dragon, standing up stiffly.

"Where is your food, dear friends? It would be nice to eat out in the open. I've been in this cave long enough."

"Absolutely! This way," says one of the elves and walks out of the cave.

Most of the spiders are gone. The elves do not see the three spiders that slip out of the cave and head as fast as they can towards Silje and Birk Witchmaster.

6

Dragons and Gray Gnomes

Tora, Wolf, and Truls stand on the grassy field in front of the cave village of Nifelheim, waiting for Sigrid.

"Let us go to the dragon caves in the mountain behind Silje and the castle," says Sigrid as she comes out to the wagons.

"Are you sure there are dragons in a cave and that they have been sleeping since Queen Ella died and the dragons lost their Dragonmaster? Tora isn't convinced. *And now I am almost grown up and can take over the role of Dragonmaster, at least that's what Sigrid thinks.* Tora is far less sure.

"Yes, of course I am sure," Sigrid laughs.

Next to Tora and Truls are four wagons pulled by large black oxen with big horns. At each ox stands a troll, holding the rope that goes to the ox's nose ring. It takes strong arms to stop the oxen if they are frightened and want to escape. The wagons are loaded with baskets filled with food for the dragons, fresh and green. No one wants to wake up dragons that have been sleeping for years without food to feed them.

"Is everything ready?" she asks the trolls.

The trolls nod.

"Wolf, I think it's best if you stay here in Nifelheim while we do this," says Sigrid. "You know how dragons feel about wolves. Come to Silje town a little later instead."

Wolf nods and walks back towards the entrance of the cave village. The trolls make a smacking sound to get the oxen walking. The oxen begin to pull and grunt with the effort to get the heavily loaded wagons to start moving. Once the wheels are rolling, things get easier, and with a creak the wagons roll onto the road through the forest.

"All right," says Sigrid. "Let's try to wake up the dragons."

The three friends follow the wagons into the shade of the trees. They don't see the two gray gnomes hiding up in the tall spruce trees. Trolgar and Botvid follow the wagons, careful not to be seen by either troll or human. Patiently, they wait for their chance to take Tora's ellacross.

The sun warms up even inside the dense forest. They decide to take a break after a few hours. The oxen are hot and tired, and the trolls unyoke them from the wagons. They lead them down to a stream where they can drink and cool off in the cold water.

Truls, Tora, and Sigrid settle down on some rocks and stretch their tired legs on the soft moss. They enjoy the bag of food they brought from Nifelheim. The trolls eat a delicate salad made of moss, mushrooms and a few occasional beetles while the humans eat sandwiches with the dwarves' golden honey. They talk about this and that with the trolls who have also settled down in the shade. The oxen stand contentedly by the wagons, ready to be on their way again soon.

"Now it's not so far away," says Sigrid. "We'll turn right when the path forks next time so we can get around the mountain to the caves."

"Oh, we're going to the dragon cave," one of the trolls growls. "I should have figured that out when I saw the plants in the wagons."

"Yes, we're going to the cave," says Sigrid. "It's time to wake up the dragons!"

"Well, it's not a day too soon," the troll grumbles and stands up. She brushes off some moss and leaves from her trousers. "Then I think we'll leave right away."

The others get up too. The oxen understand what's going on and start walking along the path themselves.

"Now they know where we're going too," says the troll, laughing. "Just follow the wagons."

Up in one of the spruces sit Trolgar and Botvid. They look at each other in surprise.

"Dragon cave?" whispers Trolgar. "What dragon cave?"

"They say there are dragons in the mountain behind Silje Castle, but I thought that was just a fairy tale," whispers Botvid. "Wow, are they going to wake up dragons? Then Birk Witchmaster is in trouble."

They look at each other and start giggling so much that they lose their balance and fall off the tree with a thud. They groan as they feel to make sure all their legs are whole after the fall. Then they get up and brush the twigs and moss off their clothes.

"Let's follow them," says Trolgar and starts walking along the small road.

"Wait, I dropped the moss that was in my nose when I fell. I'll just get a new one," says Botvid. He starts pulling large clumps of moss from the ground where Tora and the others have been resting and notices something caught in the tuft he has just pulled up.

A chain with a piece of jewellery.

"But what is this?" asks Botvid and looks curiously at the jewellery. "It smells awful!" He's about to toss it away when his friend calls out.

"Stop! It's the ellacross, Tora's ellacross," Trolgar says eagerly. "That's why it smells bad. She must have dropped it when they were resting."

"Wow, we're lucky. But what do we do now? Shall we take it to Birk?"

"No, I think we should take it to Jarl Olav," says Trolgar slyly. "I think we'll get the best reward then. Jarl Olav can be free of Birk's sorceries and perhaps even take power over both Birk and Nordanland. Then we can live like kings, you and I. And remember, they are going to wake up the dragons. Dragons *do not* like Birk Witchmaster."

The gray gnomes jump around in a ring of joy and then look at each other. With a nod, they quickly leave for the castle of Silje and Jarl Olav.

Meanwhile, Tora, Truls and Sigrid approach the dragon cave. The trolls push the wagons the last bit up the mountainside to help the oxen.

"Let's unload the wagons immediately, so we can get away before the dragons come out of the cave," says one of the trolls. They place basket after basket filled with dragon food at the cave entrance so that it will be easy to distribute the food. The trolls bow and wave and then leave with the empty carts.

Tora stands in the cave opening and looks into the darkness. She hears the breathing of large, sleeping animals and smells the pungent odour of dragon dung. The smell is not helped by a large pile of manure lying outside the cave. *I can't believe I am actually going to meet a dragon.*

"Who has been tending the sleeping dragons all these years?" Tora asks.

"Some dwarf women. They have chosen this task themselves and were taught dragon care by me and Viva. The white elves also have helped. Their queen, Nariin, can talk to dragons with thoughts when the dragons are asleep. Nariin has told the dragons what is happening. They know that we are going to wake them up and that you, Tora, are the new Dragonmaster."

"How do you talk with thoughts?" Tora asks, confused.

"You'll understand what I mean in a moment," says Sigrid, smiling. "Queen Nariin sent a message that they have found the dragon emperor Nidhugg. The elves have helped free him from the gealdor that Birk Witchmaster cast to lock him in a cave with spiderweb. Nidhugg will come to Nordanland soon."

Tora just stands and looks at Sigrid and Truls. Everything seems so strange, and no one explains anything either. *Talking in thoughts. Raising dragons. How many dragons are there? I wish grandmother was here.* Just then, a heavy sneeze is heard from inside the cave, and a gust of wind blows Tora over in the cave opening.

"Let's get going," says Sigrid and walks into the darkness, closely followed by Truls. Tora gets up, sighs, and follows Sigrid into the darkness.

7

Jarl Olav

Out in the forest by the big ditch, things have started to calm down. Mastodons and mountain giants have run away along the bottom of the ditch and disappeared towards Lake Mimir's Well. Most of the trolls also ran back when the soapy water started splashing on them. Gray gnomes and oknytt scattered in all directions as they tried to avoid being trampled. Some of Birk's army managed to get past the ditch after all and have spread throughout the forest.

Egil the Dwarf King stands looking out over the ditch. He is pleased with how it stopped Birk's army. He signals to the other leaders to gather around him.

"We won the first round, but the war is far from over. Now we must prepare quickly for Birks next attack. What do you say?"

"We've sent out a new scouting party to keep an eye on what they do next," says one of the leaders of the white elves. "Our queen has awakened the dragon Nidhugg. He is free of Birk's gealdor and on his way here."

"Good," says Egil. "Sigrid and Tora will wake the dragons in the mountain. Once they're with us, we'll have no problem winning. We must hold off the army until then and make sure Birk doesn't do too much damage. Do you have any suggestions?"

"I say we split up," says one of the dwarfs. "One part protects Nifelheim, and one part protects Silje town. Does anyone know where Jarl Olav is?" Everyone shakes their heads; no one knows.

Jarl Olav sits in the empty room of the magician Brage in the cellar of Silje Castle. Brage tried to leave a deadly gift for Viva from Birk Witchmaster, but Viva realized the gift was dangerous. She did not open it, and Brage had to leave Silje for good.

If Egil the Dwarf King had seen Jarl Olav now, he probably would not have recognized him. Jarl Olav is skinny and dirty and both his hair and beard are very long. He sits on a three-legged stool in front of the fire, chewing on mouldy bread. Around him are rats and mice waiting for him to drop crumbs they can take. Up in the castle, gray gnomes and oknytt are running around and making messes while they look for food. Everyone living in the castle seems tired and hungry.

The whole beautiful castle is now full of spiders and thick cobwebs. All the rooms are full of broken furniture and dirt, as gray gnomes and oknytt aren't exactly known for keeping order where they live. The castle servants and guards stay in rooms in the cellar and sleep most of the time. Nothing gets done.

The rat Tailtip and his cousins have moved out to the stables, where some gnomes keep order. It's warm there, and everyone gets water and food every day. The rats take it turns spying inside the castle, so they know what is going on.

Tailtip is napping on one of the ceiling beams above Jarl Olav. The room is quiet and peaceful, and the fire crackles homely. Suddenly Tailtip is awakened by the door opening with a bang. Jarl Olav is so frightened that he falls off the stool. He rigidly tries to get up from the floor and looks angrily at the two gray gnomes who have rushed in.

"What is the point of this?" he asks, trying to sound as confident and determined as ever. "Why are you interrupting my work?"

"Work?" giggles Trolgar. "You're sleeping on a stool down in the cellar. Careful you don't stress yourself out!"

The gray gnomes burst out in laughter that echoes down the cellar hallway. The spiders in the room become starry-eyed at the unfamiliar sound of laughter and start rattling around in their webs. The gray gnomes look around the room in disgust and try to wiggle some spiderwebs away.

"But, Olav, don't you ever clean anymore? Even we find this place a bit *piggy*," Botvid snorts. "Look at you! Now it's time for you to pull yourself together."

"Yes, because we have a nice present for you," Trolgar giggles and looks pleased. "Now you can take back control of Silje town and castle. We have an ellacross for you."

Jarl Olav looks curiously at the gray gnomes. He stretches a little and tries to look determined.

"Well, where did you find that cross? The last time you went for the ellacross, it didn't go so well, did it?" Jarl Olav returns stiffly to the stool and sinks down in front of the fire. *It's not worth even trying*, he thinks. *Birk would have known if there was an ellacross and taken it.* Jarl Olav takes a poker and pokes the fire with resignation.

"Stop feeling sorry for yourself!" snarls Trolgar. "Look at this!"

Trolgar holds out the ellacross so that it dangles right in front of Jarl Olav's nose. Jarl Olav can hardly believe his eyes. He follows the cross with his eyes and suddenly snatches it from the gray gnome's hand. He polishes it off with his dirty coat sleeve and then pulls it over his head. The pearl in the middle of the ellacross glitters. Gold dust rises from Jarl Olav in a swirl as Birk's gealdor disappears.

Gray gnomes look on in amazement as Jarl Olav changes completely in just a few minutes. He quickly stands up, stretches, and smiles. His hair and beard seem to shrink, and the jarl looks almost the same as before. He stretches his arms over his head and sighs.

"Oh, how nice! Now my body feels normal again. But how hungry I am! Where are my servants?" Jarl Olav looks around at the mess and dirt in the room. His face turns red with anger.

"But what is this! Are you the ones who made this mess? And whose are the spiders?" shouts Jarl Olav, narrowing his eyes at the gray gnomes.

"Welcome back," says Trolgar, nodding in satisfaction. "Birk Witchmaster took over the castle, and you, one moon-turn ago. Now he's out at Lake Mimir's Well, leading his new army in the final battle for Nordanland. I suspect he wants to take over Nifelheim and their gold too."

"Battle? What battle? Why don't I remember anything?" Jarl Olav scratches his hair in confusion. "Why do I have cobwebs in my hair?" he shouts, so that even the unseen Tailtip cowers on the rafters.

"You've been under the gealdor of Birk Witchmaster," Trolgar explains again patiently. "Now you have your ellacross, and we want our reward."

"Yes, you shall have a great reward." says Jarl Olav. "I am very grateful to you for breaking the gealdor. But first I must put things right before Birk returns with his army. Servants!" Jarl Olav rushes out of the room and heads for the stairs up into the castle.

Swiftly, Tailtip scurries off to send a message to Sigrid.

8

WAR STRATEGY

By the time the army protecting Nifelheim reaches the cave village, darkness has already descended on the forest. Many fires glow with welcome for the weary soldiers in front of the caves. Those who are not on guard eat and then go to sleep so they will be ready for tomorrow. There are soldiers everywhere, in halls, in corridors, even on the stairs. Nifelheim crouches silently in the darkness of the night, waiting for evil to reach there.

In the great hall, Egil the Dwarf King sits with other leaders discussing how to prolong the war without many people getting hurt or killed. They must buy time for Tora to awaken the dragons.

"Does anyone have a good idea? The ditch, soapy water, and smoke worked well and not many got hurt," says Egil, looking at the others around the table.

"I have a slightly different and perhaps too simple suggestion. Neither oknytt nor gray gnomes are hard to fool, as you know," says Grim Dwarf.

"Let's hear it," says Egil. "We listen to all ideas."

"Well, oknytt and gray gnomes are always hungry," says Grim, a little awkwardly. He thinks his idea is a bit lame. "They'll do almost anything for a little food, won't they?"

"Yes, that's right." The others nod in agreement.

"What do you think will happen if we hide all the soldiers inside Nifelheim where they are ready for battle? So that no soldiers are visible in front of the cave village. On the lawn in front of the caves there are many fires burning where we grill meat and sausages. We make sure that the smell of barbecue reaches Birk's soldiers long before they are here, so they have a keen appetite once they arrive. We stand in plain clothes and kindly offer them food and freshly baked bread as if it is a party."

"Yes, it will confuse them if nothing else," Egil laughs.

"Our soldiers can quickly retreat if the ruse fails. They can come through the gates and from behind the mountain through the secret passageways," says Grim.

Everyone around the table laughs and nods in agreement with Grim's proposal.

"I can already picture the look on Birk's face when he sees all the soldiers standing and eating instead of fighting." Egil laughs. "That's what we do! Let's get the ovens and fires going!"

"Atte Black Elf and I will go to Silje and see if we can help Sigrid and Tora," says Grim.

When one part of Egil's army reaches the town of Silje, the townspeople welcome them with food and shelter. Many soldiers camp outside the town walls. The many campfires and tents make a safe, glowing ring in the darkness around town. Everyone waits for tomorrow and what will happen.

Word has reached the townspeople that Jarl Olav is back to his usual self. Although he is not the best of leaders, Jarl Olav is a lot better than Birk Witchmaster. The windows of the castle show glimpses of light here and there instead of the darkness the castle had been shrouded in since Birk's arrival. Servants have been sweeping floors, fixing furniture, and cooking all afternoon and evening. But no matter how much they clean, they can't get rid of all the spiders and their webs.

Jarl Olav sits in front of the fire in the great hall on his beautiful, restored throne. He ponders how he will defend the town and castle against Birk and his evil soldiers. *How do you defend yourself against trolls and mountain giants? How will I get rid of all the spiders? Maybe it will be easier now that I have an ellacross?* Then he gets a brilliant idea. Jarl Olav stands up crossly, takes a candlestick in his hand, and walks with determined steps towards the stairs and Brage's room in the cellar.

The light flickers against stone walls and cobwebs as he walks through the empty corridor. He opens the door and enters the old healer's room. He firmly pulls the thick door shut so that the thunder echoes through the cellar vaults. He lights a few torches along the walls and walks over to Brage's bookshelf. Jarl Olav sweeps away the cobwebs covering the books and begins to read the book titles silently to himself.

"Maybe this one?" Jarl Olav murmurs, pulling out a thick book with a brown leather cover that looks like it has been read many times. "*Gealdors for Those Who Can't Be Bothered to Read Too Much Text*—perfect! A book for me, plain and simple." Jarl Olav sits down at the table and starts reading the table of contents in the book.

"ABC powder, cure headaches, love potions … let's see … cobwebs! Maybe here." Jarl Olav begins to read the book as the candle on the table slowly burns down.

After an hour or two of reading, he stretches his stiff joints and yawns loudly. Now he's ready to try his hand at magic with the help of the ellacross. First, he must find crumbled goat's tail and dried dragon's scale. Then he will say the gealdor that makes the spiders, and their webs disappear from the castle.

He searches through the jars and bottles that Brage has stored on shelves around the room. He soon finds what he needs and happily pours both ingredients onto a small wooden platter. He mixes the things carefully, but nothing happens. It just lies there like gray powder on the wooden dish.

Jarl Olav holds the ellacross in one hand, and with the other stirs the powder as he chants:

With some dragon scale

and an old goat's tail,

keep the spiders at bay,

make the web go away.

But nothing happens. Brage's room is just as full of spiders and webs as it was a minute ago. Jarl Olav sighs and thinks he may have understated the gealdor. He says it again, this time in a very loud voice. Nothing happens. On his third try, Jarl Olav spins the ellacross over the powder just in case, but nothing happens.

"Rubbish," shouts Jarl Olav, angrily throwing the powder across the room.

Then it crackles, and the powder goes around in a swirl. Jarl Olav hurries to say the gealdor again, just to be on the safe side. The powder moves faster and faster and the ellacross starts to feel warm around Jarl Olav's neck.

Bang! All the spiders and cobwebs explode with a bang so loud it wakes everyone in the town. The castle is filled with sparkling gravel that slowly rises. Then all gravel floats out through doors and windows and disappears into the dark night sky.

Jarl Olav is left sitting on the floor where he has fallen after the bang. He looks around the room. *They are gone! All the spiders and webs are gone.* He chuckles contentedly and gets up. Jarl Olav takes the book under his arm and walks out of the room to see what the rest of the castle looks like.

All the cobwebs are gone and not a spider is to be seen. Jarl Olav walks contentedly to his throne in the great hall and sits down by the fire. He opens the book again.

"Let's see if there's anything about how to win a war in here," he mutters to himself as he turns the pages.

9

Dragon Cave

Tora follows Sigrid and Truls into the darkness. The heavy breathing of the dragons echoes between the walls of the passage into the great cave. The smell of dragon manure gets stronger. Once they're a little way in, torches line the walls at regular intervals, and their light sparkles and shimmers on the walls in a way Tora has never seen before. She stops and feels her hand along the cool stone wall. Then she sees why it glitters. The stone of the cave walls is embedded with gold.

Truls has stopped and is waiting for Tora. "Yes, it's gold," he says. "Dragons only live in caves with gold. They love gold."

"Oh, it's beautiful," Tora says, caressing the gold-speckled wall once more before she starts walking again.

The walk ends abruptly, and Tora walks out into the biggest cave she has ever seen. The roof is so high that it is invisible in the dark, and the cave is so expansive that the dwarfs who work there get around on scooters.

The dwarfs that take care of the dragons have gathered around Sigrid, and they chat about the dragons and how they are doing. Tora walks up to greet them and introduce herself. The dwarfs spot her, fall silent, and bow deeply.

"Greetings, Dragonmaster," says one of the dwarfs.

"Greetings," says Tora. "Friends, please don't bow to me."

The dwarfs straighten up again. "The dragons have begun to wake up," says one of the dwarfs. "It may take a while, but they're starting to move."

"That's great," says Sigrid. "Then I don't have to wake them up with a gealdor. It's probably the dragon emperor, Nidhugg, calling."

Just then a very loud sneeze echoes through the cave. Tora is so frightened that she falls over. Two dwarfs rush forward and help her back up.

"They always have a bit of a cold when they wake up," explains the dwarf. "It will pass in a couple of days."

Tora looks around. There are five dragons in the cave. They are much bigger than she thought, and they are in different colours. Tora can see that the dragons are blue, red, green, pink, and orange even if it is rather dark in the cave. The red dragon is lying on its back with its legs in the air, just like dogs usually do. It snores loudly and occasionally smacks.

"This dragon is a bit more tired than the others," laughs one of the dwarfs. "But I'll get her going too."

"Her? How do you know if a dragon is male or female?" Tora asks, looking curiously at the sleeping dragon.

"You'll only know if the dragon chooses to tell you," the dwarf says. She grabs her scooter and glides quickly away to the snoring dragon.

The dwarf climbs onto the rock on which the dragon is lying. She lifts one of the dragon's ears hanging down over its eyes. She holds up the big ear and screams, "If you don't wake up now, I'll kiss you!"

Tora giggles. She would never have thought of saying that, but it works. The dragon stops snoring. She stretches her legs, yawns loudly, and rolls over onto her side. The dwarf must jump down quickly to avoid being pinned under the dragon's legs. The dragon smacks a few times and then opens one eye wide. She spots Tora and quickly lifts her head. Tora suddenly hears a dark voice inside her head.

Greetings, Dragonmaster Tora! You are most welcome to our cave.

Tora stands perfectly still. The dragon has not moved its mouth, and yet she hears the dragon's voice clearly in her head. She doesn't know how to respond.

You may answer me with your thoughts, says the dark dragon voice. *I hear what you think.*

Can everyone hear what you're saying? Tora thinks in return.

No, only some, replies the dragon. *You're the Dragonmaster, so you can hear me. Now let's wake up the other sleepyheads. Wake up, friends! Tora is here.*

The other dragons slowly rise. They stretch their legs and wings and yawn loudly. Then they look at Tora and bow deeply.

The dragons have long necks with large heads. Some dragons have long, hanging ears. Some have slightly smaller ears that stand up. Each has a narrow braided beard with a small gold bell at the bottom that jingles in a beautiful, brittle tone when a dragon moves its head.

Dragon eyes are quite narrow and warm golden-yellow in colour, and they have long black eyelashes. Their bodies and legs are large and covered in scales that shimmer in beautiful colours with hints of gold. The wings are large with a claw at the tip. The dragon that woke up first is a beautiful green colour that changes slightly as she moves.

"My name is Crimson," the dragon's voice rumbles in the cave. "I speak now as you do so that all will hear what we say."

"I am Bluetooth," says the dark-blue dragon, smiling broadly. Then Tora sees that some of the dragon's teeth are blue. "I accidentally bit an octopus on the butt one day. My teeth turned blue from the octopus ink," the dragon explains, laughing so loudly that pebbles fall from the cave roof.

"My name is Fire," says the orange dragon, coughing. Flames shoot out of the dragon's mouth, and the dwarfs barely have time to jump away. "Oh, sorry!"

"Oak at your service," says the red dragon and bows.

"Just me then," says the bright-pink dragon. "My name is Sable."

The other dragons laugh at the name, and Sable glares at them.

"Hello, everyone," says Tora, waving a little because it's hard to know how to greet dragons. "How come your name is Sable, if you don't mind me asking? You are not black?"

"Because I was black when I was born. When I shed my skin for the first time, I turned pink," the dragon mutters sourly as the other dragons try not to laugh.

"Glad you're awake, my friends," says Sigrid. "As Queen Nariin has told you, Birk Witchmaster is back in Nordanland and trying to take power. We really need your help."

"Absolutely," says Crimson. "We will do what Tora wants us to do." She hesitates. "But we're pretty hungry."

"Breakfast is served outside the cave," says Truls. "Jungle flame, burning nettle, and dragon lily, green and fresh."

"Yum," says Fire and immediately starts walking out of the cave. "I'm so hungry I could devour a troll." The other dragons quickly follow into the sun.

10

Breakfast

The dragons have eaten a hearty breakfast and are stretching out in the sun. Their legs and wings are a bit stiff after sleeping so long, but now they are eager to stretch their wings and fly in the sun.

"It's good if people don't know you've woken up just yet," says Sigrid. "Perhaps you could fly low along the valley towards the lake. Then the mountain and the forest will obscure you from view, and Birk and anyone at Silje won't see you coming."

"Absolutely," growls Crimson, stretching her wings to their full length.

Tora stands silently looking at the big animals, thinking it's lucky they're on her side.

Yes, you're absolutely right, she hears a dragon's voice in her head. *Do you want to fly?*

What? Who's talking to me? Tora wonders. She realizes that it will take time to get used to the dragons hearing everything she thinks.

Sable, says the pink dragon, walking up to Tora. The big dragon lies down on the ground. *Grab the hair along my neck and pull yourself up.*

Tora hesitates at first. She doesn't know the dragon and she has never flown. *Do I dare ride a giant fire-breathing dragon?*

I think so, says Sable. *Come on, get up. It's always the worst the first time you do something scary. I promise to be careful.*

Tora grabs the thick dark-pink and silver hair that grows along the dragon's neck almost like a mane on a horse. She swings one leg over to the other side and straddles the dragon's back tightly. She takes a firm grip on her hair as the dragon gently rises.

All right, Sable says. *Don't worry, I promise to fly slowly.*

Sable takes a few steps forward and stretches out the huge wings. With a powerful movement, they lift off the ground and rise gently above the treetops. The other dragons follow, and soon they are making tricks in the air, happy to be awake again. Tora enjoys the rush of the wind in her face and the incredible view of the beautiful scenery of Nordanland. Far off in the distance, the sun glistens in a large lake. *It would be so nice to take a dip*, Tora thinks.

Okay, let's fly to the lake then, says Sable and makes a couple of strong flaps of her wings to get up to speed.

The other dragons immediately follow. Like in a fairy tale, the five dragons fly over the forest, so low that the trees sway in the wind as they pass. Sable and Tora fly ahead and soon she can see the waves on the lake. Sable dives down towards the surface of the water, letting the feet drag on the surface, creating large waves. As they round a large island in the middle of the lake, they see a rowboat below. An elderly man sits fishing and enjoying the tranquillity, which is broken suddenly by five dragons flying around the island.

Oops! Sable thinks. *That's not good. Sigrid didn't want anyone to see us.* The dragon lifts quickly so as not to overturn the man's small boat, but the boat bobs up and down and the man clings to the boat for all he's worth.

We'd better fly another lap and make sure he hasn't fallen out of the boat, Tora thinks.

Okay, says Sable, making a wide turn and slowing down so as not to scare the man even more.

The lake calms down again. The man adjusts his hat and looks up at the dragon. He waves happily and calls out, "Welcome back, dragons! We've missed you!" He smiles broadly and lifts his hat in greeting. Tora laughs and waves back.

Sable returns to the dragon cave where Sigrid and Truls are waiting. The dragons land softly and smoothly on the field in front of the dragon cave. They walk up to Sigrid and Truls, who are sitting on a rock shelf, resting in the sun.

"It was nice to stretch my wings," says Crimson with a rumbling dark voice. The dragon stretches her long neck with satisfaction.

"Yes, it looked lovely," says Sigrid. "I hope no one saw you."

"Well, you never know," Oak replies, shaking her big body so that the dust drifts around.

"Okay," says Sigrid. "Truls stays here at the dragon cave. Just let Truls know if you need anything. The trolls will bring fresh food every day, so please don't eat them. I ask you to wait here until Tora calls you."

"I've been talking to Emperor Nidhugg as we flew," says Crimson. "He's on his way, but he'll fly over Lawland first. He'll be back as soon as he can after that. He's very angry with Birk Witchmaster, who apparently tricked him with cobwebs. I wonder if Birk knows that Nidhugg hates spiders?"

"Great," says Sigrid. "Then we don't have time to stand here and talk any more. Tora and I will go to Silje town to see what the situation is. Jarl Olav seems to have managed to remove Birk's gealdor over the castle. Tailtip sent me a message that everything is going back to normal. I wonder how Jarl Olav did that? It was a strong gealdor that Birk had put on the castle."

Don't hesitate to contact us. Remember, Tora, all you have to do is think of us and we'll be there as soon as we can, Tora hears Bluetooth's voice in her head.

"*Thank you, it feels safe,*" Tora thinks, and the dragons nod at her.

"Let's go," says Sigrid. "Call us if there's anything, Truls."

"Yes, but I think I can do this. It's only five little dragons, isn't it?" Truls laughs.

Fire shoots a huge flame straight up into the air, just because a dragon can. Truls is so startled that he sits on his butt.

11

Silje Town

Sigrid and Tora walk briskly around the mountain towards Silje town as the sun begins to set and night creeps ever closer. Soon they see the campfires around the town and all the soldiers sitting around them. They greet everyone they meet kindly as they slowly make their way through the camp outside the town. They are going to see the leaders of the army and hear how they intend to defend the town.

Inside the large Quacking Duck Inn on the square in Silje, the leaders are seated around a table. They are having an eager discussion over a large map of the town. Sigrid and Tora walk up to the group.

"Hello there," says Grim cheerfully. "Welcome to the town of Silje. How have you been today?"

"Hello, everyone," says Sigrid, nodding amiably to everyone around the table. "Thank you, it went well. Everything is in order."

"That's fine, but sit down and I'll get you some food," Grim says. "You look like you need it." Tora and Sigrid sit down at the table, tired and hungry, and gratefully accept the food.

"You probably have heard that Jarl Olav has taken over the castle again," says Atte Black Elf. "We don't really know how it happened, but all reports from the castle say the same thing."

"I know," says a voice from the floor. Grim bends down and gently lifts Tailtip onto the table. The rat bows in greeting. Sigrid moves her hand and mumbles a gealdor. Now everyone at the table can understand the rat. Tailtip clears his throats so that he can speak loudly enough for everyone around the table to hear him. "The gray gnomes Trolgar and Botvid arrived with an ellacross, which they gave to Jarl Olav. The gray gnomes will live as kings in the castle for the rest of their lives as payment for the ellacross."

"An ellacross?" Sigrid says in surprise. "Where does it come from?"

Tora immediately feels for her ellacross hanging around her neck. To her surprise it is gone. She grows cold with fear and feels in all pockets, but no ellacross. Then she remembers and rummages through her bag in a panic. She feels around, and all the ellacrosses Viva gave her are still there, so she calms down a bit.

Sigrid and the others sit quietly, watching Tora's panicked rummaging through her clothes. Everyone understands which ellacross it is that the gray gnomes have found.

"I … I must have dropped the ellacross when we went through the forest to the cave," says Tora, feeling ashamed as she never has before.

"Yes, that's probably it," sighs Sigrid. "Well, no point crying over spilt milk—or dropped ellacrosses, for that matter. Maybe you were meant to lose it so that Jarl Olav could gain the strength to break Birk's gealdor. Who knows how the god Odin thinks?"

Tailtip walks over to Tora and pats her hand comfortingly. She smiles back littlewanly. She's never felt so stupid and clumsy as she does right now.

"Well, then we know. Thanks, Tailtip," says Grim. "Can Jarl Olav cause us problems now that he has an ellacross?"

"No, he must know gealdors and how to say them exactly right," Sigrid says. "I can't imagine that Birk has left his books in the castle."

No one remembers Brage's room in the cellar, where he left all his magical things behind as he fled Silje town—no one, that is, but Tailtip.

"Excuse me," says the clever little rat. "Jarl Olav has been sitting in magician Brage's room for hours and hours. Aren't there books of gealdor for all sorts of things?"

The people around the table fall silent and look at one another in fear. Brage had his own magic supplies and books down in the cellar! Books and dried mushrooms, ground dragon ears and smoked pig's snout, yes, everything you could need as a magician.

"Tailtip, can you ask your friends at the castle to remove all the books that Jarl Olav might use from Brage's room?" asks Sigrid.

Tailtip nods and rushes off towards the castle as fast as he can.

"We'll have to take care of Jarl Olav if he gets up to any mischief," says Sigrid. "But first we have Birk and his new army to take care of. Now I want to know if you have come up with a plan to defend the town."

"We haven't come up with anything really good that saves lives and doesn't destroy so much, unfortunately. Whatever we do, people will get hurt or killed and parts of Silje will be left in ruin," sighs Grim. "Since they have mountain giants and mastodons, we don't have much to stop them."

Tora can hardly think about how much destruction mountain giants and mastodons could wreak on the town. No human, dwarf, or elf can stop a mastodon when it's decided to go.

Tora, Tora hears a dark voice in her head. *Can you hear me?*

Yes, thinks Tora.

This is Dragon Emperor Nidhugg. I'm on my way but heard your thoughts on the defence of Silje. What people don't know about mastodons is that they're very afraid of mice and rats. Perhaps that's something you can use in defence until I get to you?

Thank you! Great! I'll tell the others right away.

Good. The voice goes away. Tora smiles broadly.

"Well," says Sigrid, looking at Tora. "I guess you just got a message."

"Yes, Nidhugg says mastodons are very afraid of mice and rats." Tora laughs, thinking of the enormous animals flee in panic from small mice.

The others sit quietly at first and watch her, then they start to laugh.

"Well, if there's one thing they have in Silje town, it's mice and rats," says Atte Black Elf. "Let's find some of our little friends and ask them to help tomorrow." Atte and Sigrid set off into the night to ask the town's small inhabitants for help. The others remain around the table and continue to discuss.

Tora suddenly freezes again with a thoughtful look. Tora stands up and says, "I must go now. It is time."

"Yes," says Grim. "Just take care of yourself."

Tora nods and hurries down from the rooftop, running across the square towards the castle.

"Birch soap and water worked well at the ditch. I suggest we use it here against the trolls as well," says one of the leaders.

"Great, can you arrange it?" Grim asks.

"Absolutely." The leader immediately goes off to get leather bladders to be filled with soapy water. They also need to build big throwing machines to shoot them, and time is short.

"That leaves the oknytt and the gray gnomes," sighs Grim. "They've learned their lesson well, stuffing their noses full of moss against all the smells we can think of to spoil their day. Let's not forget the mountain giants either. So, what do we do?"

Suddenly the door to the inn is flung open with a bang, and two teenage boys burst in. They stare around wildly, spot the leaders, and quickly make their way to the table. They throw some sticks on the table and look very pleased.

"Hi guys," says Grim. "What's the excitement?"

"We have just returned from a long journey in the south. We hear that Birk's army will probably attack us tomorrow. Is it true?" one of the boys asks breathlessly.

"Yes, that's right," says Grim.

"We came across these bangers when we were travelling and thought they might be helpful," says the other guy. "If you come out with us, we'll show you how they work."

Grim picks up one of the sticks and smells it. The stick smells a bit acrid and weighs almost nothing. They follow the boys out into the almost empty square.

"We'll probably wake up half the town now, but we don't have time to wait until tomorrow, do we?" says one of the guys, eager to show them.

"Okay, show us what this little stick can do," says Grim.

The guys insert a short, stiff wire into one end of the banger. Then they light the wire. It sparks and burns, and the guys throw the stick well out into the square. Nothing happens.

"Okay, thanks guys for trying—" Grim starts to say. He is interrupted by a huge *bang* as the banger explodes and echoes around the houses.

They all stand gaping in amazement with ringing ears. They have never seen anything like it. Where the banger exploded, it has left a pit big enough for a gray gnome to fall in.

"Did we say we have ten boxes of bangers?" laughs one of the guys proudly.

12

Birk's Plan

Birk has climbed down from the top of the spruce tree, where he ended up when the mastodon threw him off and fled in panic into Lake Mimir's Well with the other mastodons. He walks slowly towards the lake. Birk has learned that Jarl Olav has received an ellacross and therefore succeeded in removing the gealdor over the castle. Now Birk has to try gather what's left of his army and prepare for another attack so he can take back the castle and Silje. He is convinced that he will succeed this time with the help of the blood moon.

Birk once again sits high above his soldiers in the throne on the mastodon's broad, hairy back. With a lash of his whip, he commands the mastodon, and the animal trumpets loudly in pain from the whip. The beast's sides are covered in white scars from all Birk's lashes. The mastodon swings his big head irritably so that his trunk almost snaps at Birk. Another rap, this time on the trunk, makes the animal stop.

Birk clears his throat and shouts, "Soldiers!" But no soldiers will listen to him anymore. They don't want to be forced back into the forest and ditch again. They want to live in peace and avoid fighting. Birk understands that he is losing his army and raises his wand. He points it over the great army and shouts,

"To Valhalla we go!

The enemy we will beat.

Victory will be ours.

Now move your feet."

Birk sweeps the staff over the army, and a fine gold dust falls on the soldiers. The gealdor spiced with fairy dust works instantly. The trolls stretch, the mountain giants summon the mastodons, the oknytt and gray gnomes rise and prepare. All are as eager to get going as they were at the last attack. Birk looks around with satisfaction.

"Tonight, the moon shines blood red over the forest. It is time for us to take over Nordanland and Nifelheim," Birk shouts in a dark and determined voice. "By the light of the moon, you will quietly sneak through the forest. Half of you will go to Nifelheim and hide, ready to strike at the first rays of the sun. The rest of you will sneak to the town of Silje and hide in the forest around it. When you hear my signal, you will attack both Nifelheim and Silje at the same time, so that we create confusion and panic. Rest now and leave when night comes. Go quietly and let no one see you! Victory is ours!"

Birk raises his arms above his head in a victory gesture. All the soldiers shout and jump, convinced that they will win this time. Birk already feels the warmth of victory in his stomach. He can't help but think of all he will do as king of Nordanland. The first thing he'll do as king is throw Tora into the smallest, darkest dungeon he can find, he thinks contentedly.

Birk brings his arms down and is about to sit down when the mastodon takes a wrong step. Birk loses his balance for a second and is about to fall off. "Stupid animal!" he shouts angrily and lashes the poor animal several times. "I will slaughter you when I am king!"

The big, friendly mastodon has had enough of Birk and his whip. The beast starts running towards the lake. Anyone in his way is thrown to the side. The mastodon wades into the lake as Birk screams and lashes out. He is desperately trying to hold on to the throne, which sways from side to side now that the beast doesn't care to walk softly.

A little way out in the lake, the mastodon stops, sticks his trunk in the water, and drinks for a long time.

"Stupid animal! Do you have to drink right now?" Birk shouts and stands up on the animal's back. He raises his arm to strike the poor animal once more, but that is a mistake. The mastodon lifts his trunk out of the water and quickly bends it up and back over his head, taking careful aim. Then he sprays a hard stream of cold water straight into Birk's head. Birk, unprepared, is pushed up out of the throne and down the mastodon's backside. As Birk comes sliding down, the animal kicks Birk away as hard as he can. Birk takes off with a shrill scream and lands with a splash a short distance out in the lake.

As Birk tries to swim ashore, the mastodon walks away with a satisfied rumble. The animal rips off the throne with his trunk and throws away the chair, which breaks into a thousand pieces upon a large rock on the shore. The rest of the mastodons trumpet loudly, pleased with Birk's involuntary bath. Calm settles again around the lake. No one helps Birk, who finally manages to get ashore, tired and cold.

Up in the treetops, the elves in the scouting party have seen everything and are trying not to laugh too loudly. A couple of elves leave to announce that the army will be moving during the night. Birk has once again used magic to get the soldiers to do what he wants. The sun slowly sinks behind the mountains, and the red blood moon rises for the last night this time.

13

The Attack on Nifelheim

Wolf stands and peers into the forest. He smells the acrid smell of gray gnomes, oknytt, and trolls heading for Nifelheim. Some of the elves of the scouting party follow the army through the forest. Everything seems to be going according to plan. In the part of Birk's army that is heading towards Nifelheim are oknytt, gray gnomes and trolls. The mountain giants with their mastodons have headed for Silje. Presumably Birk wants to make a grand impression riding a mastodon when he enters the town with his army.

Fires are burning all over the field in front of the cave village. The barbecue glow spreads warmth to the night watchers. It's almost time to start loading up on meat. The smell of the food must have time to spread through the forest before the sun comes up. Inside the large kitchen, dwarfs have been baking bread half the night. The smell of freshly baked bread hangs heavy over the courtyard.

Large fans have been made from cloth and branches to help bring the smell of food into the forest. They hope the smell will make oknytt and gray gnomes very hungry long before they arrive at the cave.

Morning is approaching, and it's time to spread the smells of barbecue into the forest. Meat is placed on the hot grill grates, and soon the smell of food begins to waft in. The dwarfs help each other by sweeping their fans back and forth behind the grills, spreading the smells further and further into the forest.

Wolf feels his stomach churn with hunger but decides to wait until the battle is over before eating. He wonders where Tora is. He doesn't feel good that they've split up, but he didn't have much choice. *Unfortunately*, he thinks, *dragons tend not to be too fond of us wolves. Well, I'll have to make himself useful here at Nifelheim instead.* Wolf slips into the darkness of the forest on another scouting run.

Soon he smells the dirty gray gnomes and oknytt. He crawls forward on his belly for the last bit. In a clearing in the forest, a band of Birk's army sits waiting for morning and the signal to attack.

"It's so boring just to sit here," sighs Rig, the gray gnome, throwing a pinecone at his friend.

"But stop it, you glutton hog," snarls Sigfyr who was hit. "Don't you have anything better to do?"

"I wouldn't be throwing pine cones at you if I had," replies Rig, throwing another cone.

The gray gnome gets very angry and rushes up, ready to throw himself over his friend to teach him a lesson.

"Stop," a troll snarls, lifting the gray gnomes, each by one leg. They hang helplessly, dangling some distance from the ground. "Can you smell it?"

"Yes, sorry," says Rig. "I haven't showered in a couple of days."

"Days!" chuckles Sigfyr. "A couple of years is more like it. Do as I do, and stick moss up your nose. It helps." The gray gnome points to the big tufts of moss hanging out of his big nose.

"No, it smells … it smells like bread!" The troll sighs hungrily. "Oh, how nice to have freshly baked bread this morning. It's been a long time since I've had anything good to eat."

"Us too. We're hungry," the others complain.

"My stomach is growling with hunger," whines an oknytt in despair.

They sniff and sniff the air, and indeed it smells like freshly baked bread. Then one of the trolls stands up and points a dirty finger into the air.

"Now it smells like grilled meat!" the troll almost shouts. "Do you smell it?"

"Yes! Yes!"

Everyone in the clearing stands up and sniffs the air in despair. Gray gnomes pull out the tufts of moss so that they too can smell the bread and meat. They try to figure out where the smell is coming from.

"From there," says one of the trolls firmly, pointing his big index finger at Nifelheim. "Shall we go that way?"

"Towards Nifelheim? We mustn't attack before Birk's signal!" stutters an oknytt in fear. "Birk might get angry."

"Yes, but we're hungry," a troll growls. He starts walking towards the cave village.

"We're not going to attack yet," says another troll, and starts walking too. "We're just having breakfast. Then we can go back and wait for the signal."

"Yes, that sounds like a good plan," says Sigfyr, following the trolls.

The others look uncertainly at one another in the clearing. Then they hungrily follow the others towards the dwarf stronghold. Wolf shakes his head at how gullible they are, but he's pleased that the plan seems to be working. He quietly slips back to Nifelheim through the forest as it grows lighter.

When the hungry and thirsty oknytt, trolls, and gray gnomes start coming out of the forest in a torrent, the big field in front of the dwarfen cave fills with bustling activity. Dwarfs, elves, and humans serve food as fast as they can. Soon one part of Birk's army is sitting around eating breakfast.

Egil the Dwarf King can't help but laugh at the sight. "Let's hope there's enough food for everyone," says Egil. "Otherwise, there could be trouble. But we'll give them as much food as they want. If we're lucky, they'll fall asleep when they're full. Come on, we'd better help distribute the food."

14

Jarl Olav and the Ellacross

While the oknytt, gray gnomes, and trolls eat breakfast at Nifelheim, Tailtip is sitting on a rafter in the great hall of Silje Castle. The rat looks down at Jarl Olav sitting on his throne. Jarl Olav is reading with interest the magician Brage's book *Gealdors for Those Who Can't Be Bothered to Read Too Much Text.* Tailtip silently swears to himself. He didn't get there in time to take *all* Brage's books away. But meanwhile, down in Brage's room, Tailtip's friends are dragging away as many books as they can to hide them further down in the cellar.

Jarl Olav stretches his arms over his head and yawns loudly. He looks pleased, and Tailtip realizes that Jarl Olav has found some gealdor he can use. The question now is what Jarl Olav has found. With an ellacross around his neck, he may be able to make most gealdors work. Tailtip sighs and continues to peer silently down into the great hall.

Jarl Olav stands up and stretches his body contentedly. He is stiff from hours of sitting and reading, but now he knows what to do if Birk returns to the castle. Now all he has to do is go down to Brage's room and get some dried rat-tails, ground deer antler, roasted fleas, and some ground cardamom. He's ready to defend himself. *I won't be bewitched again.* The book he found in Brage's room contains a gealdor to protect against various kinds of enchantments. Now he can only hope that with the ellacross, he will be able to make a gealdor strong enough to stand up to a wizard as powerful as Birk.

Jarl Olav hurries down the stairs to Brage's room and throws open the door. He stops at the door and looks into the room in surprise. There are rats, cats, mice, dogs, and even a couple of foxes busily moving about the floor. The animals are all working together, pushing books with their paws or carrying them in their mouths. Them seem to be heading out of the room with them. Jarl Olav is struck dumb with amazement. He has never seen anything like it. The animals stop for a brief second when they see Jarl Olav in the doorway. Then they continue to drag books out of the room between Jarl Olav's legs.

"But what's going on here?" Jarl Olav says in a weak voice. "What's going on? Why are you taking the books?"

Two foxes, each with a book in its mouth, lunge toward the doorway. Without thinking, Jarl Olav backs away and holds the door open for them.

"Here you go," he says politely. "Wait! What is this?" he shouts, making the cellar echo.

A large raven comes flying through the cellar and lands softly on Jarl Olav's shoulder. "Hello," says the bird in a raspy voice.

Jarl Olav flinches and tries to shoo the big bird away. He believes neither his eyes nor his ears. Had he not known better, he would have thought the bird was saying hello to him.

"Hello, Olav," the bird says again. "What's up?"

"H-hello," Jarl Olav stutters quietly, staring in panic at the beautiful raven with the wise eyes.

"I can say hello from Odin," says the raven.

"W-who? The *god* Odin?" stutters Jarl Olav.

"Yes, the Asgardian," says Soot, almost smiling at Jarl Olav's look of panic. "My name is Soot."

"Okay," says Jarl Olav weakly. Then he falls unconscious straight onto the cellar floor.

Tailtip comes running and scampers up to sit on Jarl Olav's chest. "Wow, he took off so fast I couldn't keep up," he gasps breathlessly. "Hey Soot!"

The raven bows in greeting. "My friends, listen! I just got word that all the mice and rats are wanted in the square. Apparently, it's really important, but I don't know any more than that," Soot finishes.

"We'll take care of the last books," says one of the cats as the others meow in agreement. "You go on to the square."

"And I'll come with you," says Soot, "to see what fun they've got planned now." He wings ahead to the square.

It takes an hour for Jarl Olav to wake up in the cellar. He slowly sits up and looks around in confusion. At first, he can't remember what happened or even why he is in the cellar. Then his memory comes back. He looks around in panic but sees neither a raven nor any animals carrying books.

"Oh, what a silly dream," Jarl Olav says to himself with a giggle. "I must have had too much wine last night. Talking ravens, and cats and mice are friends—and read books!" Jarl Olav laughs out loud.

He gets up and goes into Brage's room, then looks around, gaping in surprise. Not a single book is left on the shelves or on the table. There are some papers on the floor, and something black glinting in the candlelight. Jarl Olav bends down and picks it up curiously. It is a shiny, black, beautiful feather. Jarl Olav looks around at the empty bookshelves and then at the feather in his hand. He faints again.

15

Attack and Defence

The market square in the middle of Silje is teeming with rats and mice. In the darkness of the night, it looks like the pavement itself is squirming. In the middle of the mess, Sigrid, Grim, and Atte Black Elf stand laughing in amazement. The commotion has also brought some of the town's merchants out into the square, shaking their heads at the masses of rodents that have gathered: tiny brown hazel mice, slightly larger mice, and rats galore, black or gray.

"Oh dear!" Sigrid laughs. "There are so many of you. Hey, everybody, listen up!" She claps her hands a couple of times and shouts as loud as she can to be heard over the din. "My friends," she continues when the noise dies down, "we need your help to defend the town against Birk and his army."

A faint voice nearby rises from among the small animals, but Sigrid cannot hear what it is saying.

"Would you please pick up the black rat at your feet, Grim? Then I can hear a little better what our friend is saying."

Grim looks down where a rather large black rat sits at his feet, waving up at him. He bends down and lets the rat jump up into his cupped hands, then gently lifts her up to face height.

"Hello! My name is Haze and I said," the black rat spoke up, "that we are happy to help, but what can we little animals do? We've heard that there are trolls and mountain giants in Birk's army."

"Well, Haze, you are right. There are trolls and mountain giants in Birk's army. And", she emphasizes, "mastodons." Uneasy murmuring breaks out at the ground level of the square. The mice and rats don't want to be trampled to death by mastodons!

"That's why we need your help," Sigrid explains.

"How can you possibly expect us to help against mastodons?" Haze wonders.

"Because," Sigrid says, "mastodons are terrified of you." The mice and rats murmur among themselves in a mixture of disbelief, amazement, and pride. "According to the Dragon Emperor Nidhugg, the mastodons will turn around and stampede away as soon as they see you. If you scare the mastodons away, we can take care of the trolls and mountain giants."

"We understand," says Haze, still a little doubtful. "Let us have a chat, and you'll soon have an answer."

Grim gently puts the rat back down on the square. Immediately rats and mice gather around and discuss what to do. Sigrid and Grim can only stand and wait until the discussion is over. Haze soon pulls Grim by the trouser leg as a signal that she wants to be lifted again.

"Well, now we've discussed it," says Haze. "We're happy to help. What do you want us to do?"

"We need to figure out a way to keep you hidden until the army arrives. Then you'll come out and scare the mastodons. We hope the mountain giants will leave when the mastodons do. They usually accompany their animal friends," Grim explains.

"Let's give the mastodons a present or two, shall we?" says Atte Black Elf. Everyone looks at him in surprise since the elf rarely says anything. "Doesn't everyone like presents? Especially when they come with a big surprise."

Not many people sleep in the town tonight. Those who are able and willing help prepare the town's defences while the blood moon hangs large and red in the sky. Some of the guards at the castle also help, now that Birk's gealdor over the castle is gone. They don't want Birk back as a boss in the castle.

On the wall that surrounds the town, large throwing machines have been built to shoot birch soap and water into leather bladders at the trolls. Some villagers and some of the castle's soldiers will help fire the machines when the time comes. When they finish filling the last bladders with soapy water, that part of the defence will be ready.

Out in the meadows around the town, huge boxes are being set up. Some people carry planks of suitable length while others nail them together into square boxes. Then they nail the lid which they carefully check to make sure it fits. When everyone is satisfied, the lid is taken off again and tilted against the box before they start nailing the next box together. Finally, children come and lie long, wide, colourful ribbons next to each box.

The townspeople have also been digging pits at regular intervals around the walls of the town, each large enough hold two people. They have nailed together strong wooden lids to cover the tops of the pits. The lids are covered with grass and moss so that they will disappear into the meadow. Down inside each pit, they have placed several bangers and pins to light the wire.

In the moat that winds around the city wall, sharks now swim back and forth to prevent any creature from getting over. Sigrid has used some magic but who dares to take a chance that the sharks won't bite after all? The defence of Silje is almost ready.

From one of the castle's windows, Jarl Olav stands curiously watching everything that happens. He sees people and animals scurrying here and there but can't quite figure out what they're planning. He himself has been in Brage's room, trying to get the protected gealdor he found in a book to work, but it hasn't gone so well. Twice his hair has caught fire, and the third time his hair and beard turned purple. No matter what he does, he can't make the purple colour go away. Now Jarl Olav has shaved off his beard and pulled down a hat over his hair so that no one can see the strange colour.

The gray gnomes Trolgar and Botvid enter the hall. They go to a window and look out.

"Do you know what they're planning down there?" Jarl Olav asks. "Have you heard anything?"

"They seem to think they're going to scare away mastodons and mountain giants," says Botvid, scratching his belly. "Not sure how."

"And then they'll throw soapy water on the trolls," says Trolgar, "as they did before. You know how trolls hate soap."

"Hm, clever," Jarl Olav mutters. "But what about the oknytt and your fellow gray gnomes?"

"I doubt they have a plan for that!" says Botvid confidently, now scratching his back. "You don't scare away a gray gnome with some soap and water."

Jarl Olav thinks a moment. "We should offer our help," he says, proud of his cunning idea. "We'll help defend the town and then claim compensation when the battle is over." Jarl Olav beams with delight.

"Not such a bad idea," says Trolgar. "What do you want us to do?"

"I'll go down and offer to help. You will stand on the castle wall. When I see that Sigrid's people are winning, I'll give you a signal."

"Sounds good," says Trolgar. "But what can we do when you signal? There's only two of us."

"Gather some gray gnomes and oknytt who are here in the castle. When I give the signal, yell to your friends on the field to surrender and join our side. Scream as loud as you can." The gray gnomes nod and quickly disappear into the castle to carry out his order.

Jarl Olav looks back out at the busy meadow. Long black-grey rows are advancing along the flanks of the meadows and breaking off into units that surround the boxes. *How odd!* he thinks. *Must be some kind of magic.* Then he sees something moving in the moat. *"Wait! Are there sharks in the moat?"*

By now the first rays of the sun are visible behind the trees. The townspeople and animals of Silje are getting ready to meet Birk and his army. Two people jump into each pit and pull the covered lids over them so that they are invisible in the meadow.

On the walls of the town people are ready to fling the bladders filled with soapy water. On the castle wall, a band of gray gnomes and oknytt stand ready to scream for all they're worth as soon as Jarl Olav signals.

Everyone, people, dwarfs, elves, and animals of all sorts are ready to stop Birk and his evil army.

16

Birk Is Coming

The night before, Birk had sent his army out in two directions. One part headed for Nifelheim and were to attack the cave village at daybreak, at the same time as Birk and that part of the army attack Silje under Birks command. But Birk has been delayed and arrives at Silje first a couple of hours after sunrise because he couldn't ride his beautiful mastodon. The animal kept beating him with its trunk as soon as he approached. Birk must ride a glutton hog instead. Not nearly as impressive or beautiful, but it's better than walking, even if the glutton hog smells a little bad.

The poor animal was washed and scrubbed several times before Birk thought it smelled good enough. Oknytt brushed the pig's hair as best they could and put little bells around its neck. Birk sits on a thick, colourful blanket across its broad back, trying to hold on as the big pig slowly waddles through the forest.

As Birk finally approaches the town of Silje, he catches a faint but strange scent wafting into the forest. At first, he can't quite tell what it is. Then he figures it out: grilled meat and freshly baked bread. The glutton hog lifts its snout up into the air and sniffs grumpily. Birk feels the hunger sucking at his stomach. He understands why the glutton hog wants to go towards the smell. He does too, but he resolutely digs his heels into the side of the pig, which grunts and takes a leap forward.

A troll is waiting for Birk on the path ahead. Birk pulls the reins, and the glutton hog stops, grunting.

"We are ready, King Birk," says the troll, waiting for new orders.

"Is everyone in place in the forest around Silje?" asks Birk. "What does it look like around the town?"

"Yes, everyone is in place, and everything looks the same," the troll replies, scratching his hairy ear with a thick index finger. "Well, except for the big presents they put out on the meadow for us."

"Presents? What presents?" Birk asks anxiously. "What nonsense has Sigrid has come up with now? Does she think she can pay us off with *presents*?"

"I don't know, but the mountain giants are opening them. They couldn't wait—they wanted to see what's in the packages. Typical, isn't it?" the troll scoffs.

"But they don't know what's in them!" shouts Birk.

The troll sighs resignedly and rolls his eyes. "That's why they're opening them."

Birk desperately digs his heels into the sides of the glutton hog to gallop out of the forest, but there's no hurrying a glutton hog. The pig grunts at all the kicking but starts moving forward at its usual slow pace. Birk realizes he can run faster on his own and jumps off. He runs as fast as he can with his coat flapping around his legs.

When Birk finally comes out of the forest around Silje, the meadow is already full of gray gnomes, oknytt, mountain giants, trolls, and mastodons, gathered around the large boxes decorated with ribbons that stand here and there. Some oknytt and gray gnomes have climbed up on top of the boxes, tearing at the bows. They leap off and drag away the ribbons, and the mountain giants start prying off the lids the boxes.

Birk quickly looks around and sees the troll he's looking for. "Troll!" shouts Birk, almost out of breath. "Blow—to—attack!"

The troll looks for his aurochs, but by the time he finds it and grabs his horn to blow the call with all his might, it's too late—the lids of the boxes are coming off. Birk dives to the ground and covers his head, bracing for whatever will happen next, but all he hears are disappointed and puzzled cries from around the meadow.

"Straw?"

"It's just a bunch of straw!"

"No presents?"

"Must be something fragile and valuable," says an undaunted mountain giant. He fishes around and pulls out a handful of the straw. "What's this string?" He pulls on it, and the straw falls away to reveal a large rat dangling by her tail. "Good morning, Mr Giant," Haze says, athletically flipping herself up to stand on the giant's hand. "What a beautiful morning!" The mountain giant flings her aside, squealing, "The box is full of rats and mice!"

Haze nimbly catches onto the edge of the box and swings up on his feet. "Rodents of Silje!" she shouts. "Advance!"

All the rats and mice come pouring out of the boxes. They climb through the straw and on one another and scramble up the sides of the boxes and out, screaming as loud as they can. No one has ever heard rodents make such a sound. The mountain giants begin shrieking and run so hard they make the ground tremble, pushing aside oknytt and gray gnomes and even the trolls, who fall on their big behinds.

As soon as the mastodons spot the little grey and black animals crawling all over the place, they panic. They trumpet deafeningly through their trunks, then they all turn round and stampede towards the forest again. Anyone in the way must throw themselves aside or fall under a big mastodon foot.

Birk sees the animals charging straight at him. He quickly scrambles up from the ground and looks around in despair. He rushes to the nearest tree and climbs to the top, where he clings as the mastodons thunder past below him. Birk looks out over the mess in the meadows.

At that moment, large leather bladders of soapy water begin to fly through the air. They splat on the trolls, and the soapy water splashes all over them. The trolls scream and try to brush the soapy water away, but new bladders keep coming. The trolls roar in terror and start running back into the forest after the mastodons and mountain giants.

Birk thinks the worst must be over, but when he starts to climb down, suddenly parts of the meadow move, and smoking sticks come flying out. They land on the ground, and a couple of gray gnomes each pick up a smoking stick that fell near their feet. *No, no, no, don't pick it up*, Birk thinks. They look at it curiously but decide it's just a burning stick and throw it away. Good thing, because just then the fuse burns down, and the stick explodes with a deafening bang before it even hits the ground.

More smoking sticks are flying up out of the ground and landing all around. Gray gnomes and oknytt are so surprised by the bangers that they fall all over one another, screaming desperately. A complete panic overtakes the meadow as they try to retreat. Their leader Birk, still hiding in the tree, seems to have abandoned them.

Up int the castle wall, Sigrid, Grim, Atte and Jarl Olav stand looking out over the mess. They can't help but laugh to see how well their plans have worked. Sigrid wonders where Birk is in the chaos. She sees the glutton hog he came riding in on run into the forest again, but no wizard.

"Where is Tora?" Jarl Olav asks, both curious and worried. He nervously fingers the ellacross that hangs under his shirt. It's strange that neither Tora nor Sigrid have asked for it.

"She's just picking up some old friends," Sigrid replies. "I'm sure you'll be happy when you see who they are."

"Ok," Jarl Olav says nervously. He doesn't want Sigrid to see his purple hair and pulls the hat further down over his hair.

The gray gnomes and the oknytt are standing on the castle wall waiting for a signal from Jarl Olav. When they see him pulling his hat, they think it's the signal to bring their friends in from the meadow, so they won't be harmed. They start shouting at the gray gnomes and oknytt below, jumping up and down with gestures of invitation.

Their friends down in the meadow look up in surprise at their friends on the castle wall. What in Valhalla are they doing in the castle? What do they want us to do?

It is high time for the return of the dragons.

17

Tora, Nidhugg, and the Flatfeet

Tora runs across the castle courtyard and down a cellar staircase. She continues through the long, dark cellar and further into the passageways that wind under the castle and into the mountain behind the town. Finally, the very long passage opens into the great cave where the dragons have slept for many years. The dragon Crimson inside Tora's head has shown the way. Now the dragon asks her to go outside in front of the cave.

Tora comes out from the pitch dark, breathless and barely able to see anything in the bright sunlight after the darkness in the aisles. As her eyes adjust to the bright light, she sees a very large dragon in front of her, larger than all the other five dragons. He shimmers in a beautiful shade of blue-green with splashes of gold. The dragon has a long golden beard finely braided, and bright golden-yellow eyes that look at her warmly. Tora knows immediately that here stands the Dragon Emperor Nidhugg, imposing and beautiful.

"Dragon Emperor Nidhugg," Tora greets with a deep bow.

"Dragonmaster Tora." Nidhugg bows his head elegantly. "I'm very happy to finally meet you."

"I say the same," Tora replies. "As Dragonmaster, I will need your knowledge and advice."

"It will be my pleasure to teach you everything I know about dragons," says Nidhugg with his dark rumbling voice. "But first we'll put an end to the wretched Birk Witchmaster once and for all. The blood moon is over for this time. It's time to have some peace and quiet in Nordanland again."

"How can I help?" Tora asks.

"Unfortunately, you will have to take responsibility and become Queen of Nordanland. Just as your mother was, even though you are so young. We will all help you rule the land," says Nidhugg. "Nordanland needs a wise queen. Jarl Olav can move on with his life and do something else."

"I know nothing about what a queen does," Tora says nervously. "I don't think I can."

"Yes, you can do a lot more than you think!" Nidhugg laughs. "But let's take it one day at a time. Hop on my back. We will end the war today."

"But who are all these people?" Tora asks, pointing to the creatures standing in hundreds around them.

"These are Flatfeet," says Nidhugg. "They will help bring order to Silje town. Flatfeet are experts at keeping order, in fact. They just ask people to do things in a nice way and people do. No one knows why, you just obey. I flew past them on my way here and asked them to help."

"Flatfeet?" says Tora, surprised. "I don't think I've ever heard of Flatfeet before. Or seen any."

Tora looks curiously at everyone standing around her. The Flatfeet are quite short but muscular. They all have long black hair, very blue eyes, and big ears. But the strangest thing to her is that they all look almost the same—same hair colour and hairstyle, same clothes, almost the same facial expressions, as if hundreds of siblings are standing around her.

"Where do the Flatfeet come from?" Tora asks curiously. "Since I've never met one before."

"They live far away in Lawland," Nidhugg replies. "But we don't have time to talk more now. Get on my back, and let's fly."

As Tora climbs onto Nidhugg's back, all the Flatfeet run off in perfect ranks along the small road that goes round the mountain to Silje. The other five dragons take off one by one. They circle around while they wait for Tora and Nidhugg. With a couple of mighty flaps of its great wings, the Dragon Emperor takes off.

Meanwhile, Birk settles in a little more comfortably up in the fir tree. He doesn't dare climb down quite yet. Gray gnomes, oknytt, and trolls are still milling about, but none of them knows where they are going or what to do next.

Birk sighs and wonders how it all went so wrong. He had devised a near-perfect plan to take power, and it ended in chaos. Now he can think only of the army at Nifelheim. Maybe they've managed to take over the dwarfs' cave village? He has to get there to find out. Birk looks around and spots some gray gnomes walking calmly through the forest towards Silje.

"Hey! Stop!" shouts Birk in a firm voice.

The gray gnomes Rig and Sigfyr stop and look around but don't see anyone. It's hard to hear anything because the forest is full of gray gnomes, trolls, oknytt and the occasional mountain giant, not knowing what to do next. Suddenly a glutton hog with a colourful blanket on its back comes running while the little bells around its neck jingle loudly. Rig and Sigfyr quickly jump to the side so the glutton hog can pass.

"Up here! In the tree!" cries Birk.

The gray gnomes look up and to their surprise see Witchmaster Birk.

"What in the name of Thor are you doing up there?" asks Rig "Are you playing squirrel?" The gray gnomes look at each other and burst out laughing.

"Squirrel! Birk Squirrel." The gray gnomes double over with laughter at their own joke.

"Yes, very funny," sighs Birk. "I want you to run to Nifelheim and see how the army is doing there. Then get back here as fast as you can."

"We just came from Nifelheim," Sigfyr says.

"Oh!" Birk lights up. "How did it go?"

"It went very well," says Sigfyr and nods.

"Yes, there was enough for us too, even though we arrived a little later than the others," says Rig.

"Enough? You haven't already divided up all the gold in Nifelheim?" Birk shouts in panic that he didn't get his share.

"Ha ha, you're too funny, Birk." Rig laughs. "Gold! Who cares about gold when there's freshly baked bread?"

"Freshly baked bread? What on earth are you talking about?" Birk shouts, so angry he's red in the face.

"Look," Sigfyr giggles, poking at his friends. "Now he looks more like a robin who belongs in a tree!"

The gray gnomes burst out laughing. They laugh so hard they fall over in the moss.

"Explain yourselves at once!" Birk shouts, shaking the tree in anger.

"Well, when we got there, the dwarfs had laid out grilled meat and freshly baked bread for breakfast. Very decent of them," says Rig, wiping tears from his eyes.

"We thought it would be very rude to attack them after all that good food, so we came here instead," says Sigfyr.

"But you look like you had fun here too," says Rig, pointing out to the meadows where all the brightly coloured ribbons were strewn about the opened boxes. "Let's go and have a look."

Birk slumps down on his branch and sighs deeply. All is lost. They have all outwitted him. *Freshly baked bread!* Birk suddenly feels how hungry he is.

18

An End and a Beginning

The meadows outside the town of Silje are beginning to calm down. The mice and rats have gone back for a well-earned rest to their own nooks and crannies. All the mountain giants went home, tired of Birk and his nonsense. But more and more gray gnomes, oknytt, and the occasional troll are coming out of the forest. It is the army that marched on Nifelheim and ate breakfast instead of attacking. Now full and satisfied, they have decided to come to Silje to see how the others are doing, but mostly they all sit and rest on the grass.

Egil the Dwarf King and Wolf also arrive. As they look across the meadows and wonder what has happened, there is a roar from the sky like nothing they have ever heard before. Six mighty dragons come sailing over the town.

Birk hears the dragons and looks up to see them sweep down from the sky. To his horror, he sees that Tora is riding one—and not just any dragon, but Nidhugg the Dragon Emperor! How did Nidhugg get free from the gealdor he cast? Nidhugg was supposed to slowly starve to death deep inside the cave, bond under thick spiderwebs. Birk understands now that there's only one thing he can do. Escape! Escape quickly and get as far away as he can.

Birk starts to climb down carefully from the tall tree, but it's too late. The dragons are diving down towards what's left of Birk's army and shoot metre-long flames over the tall trolls' heads. The trolls throw themselves to the ground, covering their ears and tails. At the same time Fire, the orange-yellow dragon, circles Birk's fir tree, spraying fire so that it catches fire at the top. The fire starts to spread down the trunk, and Birk has to climb faster and faster to escape it.

The dragon flies one last lap around the tree and then dives down. He easily picks up Birk with his left foot. Birk is caught helplessly within the dragon's powerful claws.

Nidhugg and the other four dragons land on the castle wall. Nidhugg looks out over the town and the meadows. Then he lets out a roar that makes everyone's blood run cold, except for Tora. She sits quietly on the big dragon, waiting for Nidhugg to signal her that it's her turn.

Just then, all the Flatfeet come running in a straight line out of the forest and line up in a ring around the town. They look determined and serious, and people move for them.

"Listen!" Nidhuggs' dark, slightly raspy voice echoes between town and forest. "Listen carefully!"

No one dares to make a sound. Everyone stands quietly and looks up at the impressive dragon on the castle wall.

"I am Dragon Emperor Nidhugg," the terrifying voice echoes around them. "I am the leader of the dragons—*and all of you.*"

Everyone bows deeply and for a long time so as not to annoy the dragon.

"On my back sits your queen, Tora," says Nidhugg. "Your queen and master of dragons."

Everyone bows once more. Wolf can't help but smile proudly at Tora sitting so safely and calmly on the big dragon's back. Egil the Dwarf King, sees Sigrid from afar and starts walking towards her with Wolf.

"This war ends now," says Nidhugg, and everyone nods in agreement. "All the fighting and bickering ends now. From now on you will live together in peace no matter where you come from. Queen Tora is a wise and fair woman who will lead the country together with a council that you all choose. My friends, the Flatfeet, will help you keep the town and forest peaceful until you have elected the council." Everyone looks at one another and nods.

"Birk Witchmaster will be exiled for the rest of his life," Nidhugg continues. "He will never be allowed to return to Nordanland. The dragon Fire will fly away with Birk and drop him on an island far away."

Fire sweeps low over the people with Birk in a firm grip. Everyone sees him caught between the dragon's great claws. After a few turns, Fire takes off with Birk and soon disappears over the mountains. Birk is on his way to the island where he will live the rest of his life, and the people sigh with relief. They must not have Birk as king.

"My name is Tora and I promise I will be a good and fair queen," says Tora, "Let's get moving and clean up all this nonsense after Birk. Jarl Olav, I want to talk to you, so come to the castle courtyard, please."

Tora climbs down from the dragon and then jumps down from the wall. *Why don't you go in the castle and change clothes? I entertain Jarl Olav in the meantime.* Nidhugg looks at Tora and then walks towards the castle's large courtyard. Tora nods and runs into the castle, her castle.

Jarl Olav looks at Sigrid with panic in his eyes. He doesn't want to go and talk to the Dragon Emperor, but he has no choice. Jarl Olav feels the ellacross hanging around his neck suddenly become warm and heavy. *I wish I had been kinder.*

"I'll go with you," says Sigrid, patting his arm reassuringly. "I'm sure you'll be fine, you'll see. The dragon is kind and fair and wishes no harm."

"Well, you're lucky, you'll not end up on the same island as Birk Witchclown." Egil pats him on the back reassuringly. "You'll be fine."

Jarl Olav is so nervous that he trips on a rock and drops his hat. The purple hair shines brightly in the sunshine. Sigrid, Egil the Dwarf King and Wolf look curiously at his somewhat strange hair colour.

"Maybe I can help you choose another hair colour when we're done here," says Sigrid, finding it hard to keep from laughing.

19

Queen Tora

Everyone gather in front of Nidhugg in the large castle courtyard. There are people everywhere, on the wall, in windows, on straw bales, even on the outbuildings' roofs. They are all curious about the beautiful dragon and what punishment the dragon and Tora will give Jarl Olav.

Jarl Olav, on the other hand, is not so curious about what Nidhugg and Tora wants to talk to him about. He walks up to the dragon trembling. He can't see Tora anywhere, but her ellacross is burning under his clothes.

With some amusement, Nidhugg silently looks at him for a long moment to make him nervous. He's toying with the jarl who mismanaged Nordanland so. He's just waiting for Tora.

The noise in the castle courtyard dies down as the castle's big doors open. Tora steps out, beautiful and elegant as only a queen can be. She wears shiny black trousers and a black-and-white polka-dot caftan over a long white shirt. She comes to stand silently on the castle steps. On her head is a beautiful black tiara with sparkling diamonds that shine in the sun.

The dragons sitting around the castle wall spread their wings, and Bluetooth calls out in a dark voice, "Long live Queen Tora!" The cheer echoes between house and forest and seems never to end. Finally, the dragons fold in their wings and take a bow. The cheer ends abruptly, and everyone bows to the woman who will become one of the most powerful queens of all time.

Tora goes down and stands next to Nidhugg. She looks thoughtfully at Jarl Olav and says: "You have something that is mine."

Jarl Olav gasps for breath as he holds tightly to the ellacross he has hidden under his shirt. "Me?" he says nervously. "I don't know what you mean." The heat from the ellacross burns his hand so he lets it go.

"Queen Tora, allow me," says Nidhugg. "Egil the Dwarf King has apparently asked the god Thor for a favour."

Egil looks at Nidhugg in surprise. Has he asked the god Thor for a favour? And how does the dragon know? Nidhugg lifts one of his wings and flicks the claw on the tip against a stone. A blue-white spark forms then travels in a small circle once around Jarl Olav before searing into his buttocks. With a shrill scream, Jarl Olav jumps around clutching his backside as a little smoke comes from his trousers.

Everyone in the castle courtyard is at first completely silent. Then all breaks into a fit of awkward laughter that reverberates between the walls. Then Egil remembers praying that Thor's lightning would pinch the enemy's buttocks. "How did the dragon know I made that prayer?" he whispers to Sigrid.

She looks at him and laughs. "Yes, you must be careful what you wish for. The gods might hear you."

"Olav, this is the last time I'll say this kindly," says Tora when the laughter has died down. "You have something that is mine."

Olav immediately takes out the ellacross, pulls it over his head, and hands it to Tora. She sighs with relief at getting the important necklace back. Now she has the ten crosses again, safe from evil powers. She immediately hangs it around her own neck. "Olav, you will stay here in the castle," says Tora.

Olav bows in thanks, happy and relieved that he won't have to leave the castle.

"For the next five years, you'll be working in the stable with special responsibility for the pigs," says Tora, finding it hard not to smile. "You start today."

"But I don't know anything about pigs," Olav protests. He has always been afraid of working.

"Are you going to learn?" Nidhugg asks as he flexes the claw at the tip of his wing.

"Absolutely," says Olav quickly, covering his buttocks with both hands. "It will be very interesting."

"Then it is decided. Tomorrow we will have a big party to celebrate that Birk and his evil magic is gone. I hope you all want to help preparing the party?"

"Yes! Yes!" The people shout and applaud.

"In the meantime, we will plan for the election to the Nordanland council. In a week every adult who wants to, vote for who will help me govern Nordanland. Now we have a lot to do. Let's go, everybody!" Tora says and starts walking towards the castle's big doors.

Inside the great hall, Tora sits on the throne for the first time. Strangely, it feels natural and right from the first moment. Suddenly she hears a voice in her head, *Welcome home, honey! I will go to Odin now. Sigrid and your friends will take care of you. I will see you in Valhalla, but not for many years to come. Be good, be strong, be wise!*

Grandma! Tears run down Tora's cheeks. She quickly wipes them away so no one will see them. *Grandma will like Valhalla*, Tora thinks. *Now is the time for us to make sure that life is good for everyone who lives in Nordanland.*

Her friends settle down at the table. The three ravens have flown in and sit in the windows, resting in the sun. On the beams under the ceiling Runar Rat and Tailtip sit and listen, looking down on the people at the table. The sun lights up every nook and cranny of the room and the fire crackles peacefully in the fireplace. You can hear people talking and laughing behind the closed door.

"Our first point will be to hold an election for the council," Tora says.

"Wait a minute," says Sigrid, holding up a hand.

She walks over to the wall and quickly sweeps down three spiders from a web. She walks over to the fireplace and throws the spiders in the fire. Tora gasps. What is she doing? Sigrid never hurts animals. The spiders go flying and disappear with a poof.

"I think those were the last of Birk's spiders," Sigrid explains. "Those three must have come all the way from the cave where Nidhugg was held. They were harmless, but now might be able to report everything to Birk on the island, so they had to disappear. Good thing they're not real animals."

They begin the work of putting Nordanland back in order. Outside the castle, humans, gray gnomes, and oknytt are cleaning up the town and meadow for the party. Soon a wonderful smell of food spreads through the castle and the town. Life has become bright again in Silje.

A man in a dark cape lingers in the shadows, curiously following everything that happens. Then he turns to walk away. For a brief second, a glimpse of a scarred, burned face appears. Wolfpelt is back.

WORDS TO KNOW

beacon	fires lit on high ground so they can be seen from far away to warn people
black elf	a tall, slender people who have long black hair and often wear black clothes
draug	an evil spirit, the living dead
dwarf	a short, strong, helpful, friendly people
ellacross	a cross with a circle in it; the wearer is protected by Odin and/or a gealdor
flatfoot	a people who are short and strong, with big ears and black hair, and who live in Lawland and are good at keeping order
gealdor	spell
giant	a big, strong, helpful people
glutton hog	a species of very large boar with bristly hair on its back, known for its ill temper
grey gnome	a short, mean, cunning people with strong muscles and a bony face with a big nose
mastodon	large elephant with furry coat and huge tusks
mountain giant	a race of mountain-dwelling giants who are very big, strong, and always angry with humans and dwarfs
moon-turn	month
Nix	a naked man who lives by the water and plays the violin so that people are attracted to the water by the music
oknytt	small, yellowish, mean creatures with long, floppy ears
pixies	**a** short, easily angered people who wear clothes that make them invisible in the wild

runes	letters carved into wood or stone, can be magical
seid	healer, magician; cures and helps the sick, can see into the future, can speak different languages and sometimes even with animals.
sorcerer	male magician with evil intentions
sun-turn	year
ting	a council where leaders gather to decide important things such as going to war
troll shot	a special gealdor that makes you sick or kills you
white elf	a very tall, slender people with long silver-white hair, often wearing white clothes

Printed in the United States
by Baker & Taylor Publisher Services